Jerome

# Jerome

## William Taylor

**alyson books**
los angeles | new york

THE ASSISTANCE OF THE WRITING FELLOWSHIP AT THE DUNEDIN COLLEGE OF EDUCATION, AND OF CREATIVE NEW ZEALAND, IN THE WRITING OF THIS BOOK IS GRATEFULLY ACKNOWLEDGED BY THE AUTHOR.

PRINTED IN AUSTRALIA.
TEXT DESIGN BY JENNY COOPER.
SIMULTANEOUSLY PUBLISHED IN NEW ZEALAND BY LONGACRE PRESS.

THIS TRADE PAPERBACK ORIGINAL IS PUBLISHED BY ALYSON PUBLICATIONS, P.O. BOX 4371, LOS ANGELES, CALIFORNIA 90078-4371.
DISTRIBUTION IN THE UNITED KINGDOM BY
TURNAROUND PUBLISHER SERVICES LTD.,
UNIT 3 OLYMPIA TRADING ESTATE, COBURG ROAD, WOOD GREEN, LONDON N22 6TZ ENGLAND.

FIRST U.S. EDITION: NOVEMBER 1999

99 00 01 02 03 a 10 9 8 7 6 5 4 3 2 1

ISBN 1-55583-512-0

*for my good friend and 'son',*
*Michael Stalder*

# MARCO PHONES KATE

'Katie! Katie! Is that you Katie? Katie it's Marco. Katie! Jerome's dead. Fuck Katie, JEROME IS DEAD!' a scream.

'Marco? Marco? I can't hear you. It's a terrible line, Marco and I can't hear. I can't understand you. What was... Start again, Marco. What are you..?' Momentary time lags mean that each talks over the other.

'He's gone, Katie. He's shot himself and he's gone. JEROME IS DEAD! JEROME IS DEAD, KATIE!'

'Marco... I can hardly hear... ' Delay. 'What about Jerome? What is it about Jerome?' she says loudly.

'Katie, Jerome went out shooting and he's shot himself and he's dead and they just told me and shit I dunno what to do... went after the rabbits all by himself and seems he tripped gettin' over a fence... Jerome never tripped over a bloody fence in his whole life... '

'WHAT ARE YOU SAYING, MARCO?' she is yelling. 'What is it? Speak slower, Marco and give some time... '

Marco speaks slowly, loudly. 'Jerome has had an accident. Jerome has gone and killed himself dead and Jesus what can I do now? What can you 'n me do now?' and then he yells... 'JEROME IS FUCKIN DEAD AND I DUNNO WHAT TO... ' Marco is gasping, gulping. He is wide-eyed. His mouth works but no sound comes. He slumps against the wall and slowly slips to the floor. His father takes the receiver from his hand, speaks briefly, hangs it up, tends to his son.

# MARCO WRITES TO KATE

Dear Katie,

Dunno where to begin. Dunno really how to write a letter! We buried him, Jerome. He's in his grave down the old cemetery and I can't get out of my mind a picture of him lying there all stiff and cold and wrapped up and in his coffin. It's one in the morning and I'm gonna get this done and fax it off to you. My head aches in behind my eyes. It's just so bad and it's getting worse because I can't lay off Jim and Jack (one shot of Jim and then one shot of Jack) and too many cigarettes – like one every ten minutes! But I'm gonna write it all down anyway. This stupid bitch of a woman – I think she was some sort of aunty of Jerome – kept asking me if I'd cried and if I'd talked and let it all out! Who to, for Chrissake? Her? There was only him I could have cried to and let it all out to! And had a laugh about it to! And he's fuckin dead, the bastard. Then there's you, but you are on the other side of the bloody world. But you're the only one and so you're gonna get it. I know you loved him and I can guess the shit you're going through and I guess I can guess how you are feeling. Guess guess guess! Three guesses! If you are feeling like me you are feeling like shit. I hope you've got a bottle of something good.

Why did it happen, Katie? Why the fuck did it have to happen? *My mate!* He's dead and gone and so is part of me and the ache and the pain is so bad and the booze and the smokes won't cover it up and I just feel so lonely and alone.

The funeral was very nice as funerals go, I guess. Dunno, do I? Never been to one before. St Mary's church was packed and there were crowds outside even though it pissed down with rain. Someone said it was the biggest fuckin funeral ever seen in Atherton. Cool, eh? Hundreds and hundreds there. The stink of all the flowers made me want to puke. Like, man, you never seen so many flowers outside a flower shop or a big garden. Horrible looking things, too, and all stinking. Helluva lot of people crying. But not me and not Jerome's olds. His mum looked zonked, completely out of it and his old man seemed to carry her most of the time. Don't think she knew where she was.

Then there was all the holy shit. Father O'Something done most of the holy shit and they even had a bishop there to give a hand on account of Jerome's old man being the mayor. Was the bishop guy got to read out your message, 'From Jerome's very close friend Kate Brown in the United States.' Jesus! From Jerome's very close friend! Man, you'd think old Jerome was up there already with Jesus and all the saints! In fact the priest guy made out Jerome had been a saint all his bloody life. I didn't know who the hell he was talking about for a bit. I thought it was something to do with Jesus but it wasn't, it was Jerome! *My mate! My dead mate!* Sure wasn't the Jerome that I knew – or that you knew! Hell, Jerome was no bloody saint. You don't get many saints goin' out with a gun to blast the shit out of a heap of God's little furry creatures. And some of the things Jerome said about poor old God and Jesus I couldn't write down! He drank, he smoked, he swore like shit, he loved shooting things that moved and God knows what all he got up to with you! He never told me stuff about that. I just bet God and Jesus are having a hard time right now working out what to do with my mate, Jerome. I do hope they give him a chance because he was a good guy, the best of mates and, like, well he was part of me and now he's gone.

Me and five other guys carried him out to the coffin wagon. Then we got to carry him again up that long winding path up to his grave in the old cemetery. You know the place. I bet he took you up there a hundred times. It's where all his old family are buried in the middle of that group of big trees. We used to shoot rabbits there all the time because Jerome reckoned cemetery rabbits were the worst and made their nests in the bones of dead people. He might've been right. Heaps of the bastards up there – dead people and rabbits!

Then we went back for the party. There was more booze than a pub and Jerome's dad told us we were brave guys and to help ourselves to the drinks and he'd see we got home safe. We sure drank a lot. Jerome would've approved of that.

Gotta go now. I am just so pissed. Dad came and got me from the party. He's cool, is Dad. He asked what I wanted to do tomorrow. I said I wanted to go for a long drive, smoke as much as I wanted without Mum nagging me and then shoot something. He said okay to it all. I'm gonna get a heap of rabbits. See I don't want them getting into the old cemetery. That'd piss Jerome off majorly, having bloody rabbits getting into his bones. He's cool, is Dad. Pity about him and Mum. Stupid guy keeps getting caught putting it away in yet another girlfriend. His latest one is only a few years older'n me. He's mad. Mum's leaving him. Dunno where I'll go.

Better fax this now while I can still use the machine. There's a lot more I could tell you but I'm just so drunk I can't. Pity you don't have e-mail where you are now. Getting okay at them on Dad's computer but reckon I'd be too pissed tonight to get one straight.

I am thinking of you, Katie. Here's to you, babe! (just mixed up half a Jim with half a Jack). On my third pack of smokes for today, too! Shit hot, eh?

Marco

## KATE WRITES TO MARCO

Marco:

Thanx for the fax. I'm a bit wasted myself but not too bad. Got to keep my wits about me in this hell-hole place. You write to me as much as you like. If it helps you just write it down. For the next three weeks or so just be a bit careful about what you put in a fax. Mind you, if you use big words they won't understand them! Only problem there, is neither will you! I'm leaving this place to go to a family in Minneapolis at the end of the month. It's a long story and it's not the time for it now. It's enough to say that no one here gives a shit that I've just lost a friend.

I knew most of what you told me about the funeral. My sister Susan phoned me right afterwards and we talked for an hour and it helped. I've been on the phone a lot to Susan. I know she can be a bossy old tart but she's really helped get me through these last few days. I sure needed to get a few things straight after that first phone call from you. Poor old Marco. D'you remember phoning? I don't think you do. You are going to miss him so much – your 'other half'. I used to laugh at the two of you. You were so close.

I am going for a long walk now down to Little Deer Lake.

It is a lovely place and sometimes, if you are very quiet, you can spot deer coming down to the edge of the lake and having a drink. They are very little deer, I don't know what sort. Very sweet. I used to think how good it was that neither you nor Jerome was here with me – all that blood lust would have been too much for me – and for the little deer! I am thinking a lot about Jerome. All the time. Well, most of the time, I guess. I loved him, too, Marco, altho' maybe not quite in the way you think.

Write to me, man. Just be careful what you say. I don't want this horrible family knowing anything more about me than they think they know already. Only three more weeks.

Cut down on the Jim, the Jack, and the smoking, Marco. None of that stuff helps. You might think that it does, but it doesn't. However, that's up to you and I guess you'll go on doing whatever you want. I am sorry about your mum and dad. These things happen – what a bloody stupid thing to say. And how on earth would I know? I haven't got either!

I know this will sound dumb to you, Marco, but would you take a flower and go up to the cemetery and put it on Jerome's grave for me? Oh, fuck, now I'm crying and I don't want to...

What do you think made him do it, Marco. What do you think?

Love,
Kate

## MARCO WRITES TO KATE

Dear Katie,

I'm writing straight back to you after what you said. Jesus, Katie, you got it wrong!

What the fuck do you mean? *What made him do it?* What are you saying? Was an accident. Bloody horrible awful accident. That's all it was. You don't know what you're talking about. Who's said stuff to you? Was it your sister? What the hell does she know? Just 'cos she runs Jerome's old man's law firm doesn't mean she knows everything. You got it all wrong, Katie. *Why did it happen?* We know why it happened. Stupid bugger was climbing a fence and forgot all the safety shit him 'n me had to learn back to front and sideways before the cops'd give us our gun licences. Just a stupid stupid accident and now he's gone for good.

Probably you meant how did it actually happen. Seems he lost his footing and slipped sort of sideways. Stupid bastard. They reckon it was very quick but I wonder how they know.

I keep seeing him. I see him in my room at nights when I try to go to sleep and he's sorta just standing there and he doesn't talk or nothing. Just seems to be standing there like he wants to say something to me. Last night I cursed him out loud. I yelled at the bastard and told him to piss off and I didn't want him haunting me and it wasn't my fault he'd bought it. Nights are just so bad. I get up, get a drink and then sit on my window-sill for an hour or two and just think and smoke.

Jerome was the best mate any guy ever had, Katie. He was. I never wanted to lose him. Him 'n me had been together all our lives and each of us seemed to know most of the time what the other was thinking. It was awesome sometimes. We'd just look at each other and we'd know what the other one was thinking. Just have to grin and wink. No one could ever have had a better mate. He was just a good decent kind guy and I'd have done anything for him and him for me. Could always count on Jerome. We were a bit like twins, I reckon. Only difference is he's blond and I'm dark. We're just the same apart from that. Same clothes and all that shit, same good habits and one or two same bad habits, think the same way.

We were just the same, Jerome 'n me, Katie. We were. I know that. I know you think I'm thick as shit. I'm not, you know.

Went up to the old cemetery like you asked and took a flower for you. Dunno what sort it was. Spotted a very nice one in next door's garden and was gonna nick that but then thought you wouldn't like it – me stealing and all. Can remember a year or so back when me and Jerome got into shoplifting bigtime and how you had his guts for garters back then and blamed me for leading him astray. Me leading him astray! We were doing quite well until you stopped us and no one but you ever knew. So I went to the flower shop down the mall and I think I got him a rose from you. Just as well he got a fresh flower because all the crap on his grave is now as dead as he is. Reckon the least they could do is see that dead people have live flowers. Kicked most of the dead shit off and put your one in the main place by the little marker that says JEROME WINTER. I think they get him a better one soon. Just a little wooden marker. Then I left. Biked down past his house. I thought I might go in. Old

Edith, Mrs Winter, was out in the garden doing something and I stopped and was going to go in. She saw me. I know she did. She looked right at me, sorta staring hard. Didn't say a word. Just looked hard and then turned away. Poor bitch. Guess she was thinking why the hell couldn't it have been me and not her boy. Dunno. Don't seem to know much at all these days.

How's it hangin with you, Katie? What's this shit you reckon you're in? I thought everything in your life was cruisy. You got to go to America the Land of the Free and all that jazz. Just what you always wanted. Jerome reckoned you were having a hot time. He told me you were even the home-coming queen or princess or something like that and every guy on the football team had only one score on his mind!

God, Katie, I am so lonely. It hurts. Write me soon.

Marco

P.S. Mum's shooting through on Friday. Fuck, she sure hates Dad. She's taking Cherie and the two cats and leaving me with Dad so my address stays the same. Guess it's okay. Had to happen. Just it seems shit happens all at once. She said I'd be better off with Dad because we're birds of a feather or something. She says the cats'd be better off with her because they wouldn't last for five minutes after she'd left! She's bloody right on that one!!! Never had very much to do with Cherie. She's only ten. But I think I'll miss her. I am so lonely, Katie. It was always him 'n me. Jerome and me.

# KATE WRITES TO MARCO

Marco:

Look, man, if it helps, just write. You write every day if you want. Forget that crap about being careful of what you say. I don't give a damn what these sods see or read. Only just over a week to go and I'll be out of here. The exchange student co-ordinator comes on Thursday next week to take me to my new family in Minneapolis. I've spoken to them but not met them. Sally and Jills. They sound so welcoming. I'll tell you more about them later. This is going to be one long letter! I'm down by the little lake. It's well into autumn but still quite warm. There's the sweetest, gentlest little terrified deer only about a hundred metres from me. God, I'm glad you're not here!! Only joking. I wish like hell that you were here!

But I don't want to joke with you, Marco. I know it's still so soon after Jerome's death. I know it's hard for you but you've got to get on with things. Jerome is dead. I read and re-read your letter, Marco, and I'm worried. I know it is quite the wrong thing to say just yet but, Marco, you have got to pull yourself together. That is the most awful thing for me to say, I know. And it is silly, but I can only hope that you know what I mean.

We both loved Jerome, Marco. We loved him a helluva lot, more than he ever deserved – and you know that, too! There! I've said it! I know we're not supposed to say bad things about the dead, but I am going to tell the truth. You called Jerome the kindest and most decent guy... That's crap, Marco, and you know it. We loved him. But let's not be blind about him. Jerome was a shit! Not always, I know – he was my mate, too. But you and him, Marco. God, two little rich boys who always got everything you wanted. Okay, that's a bit of a low blow, I know. Maybe you weren't as rich as all that but it was a helluva lot more than I ever had! Susan had to take out another mortgage on our house to pay for me to get here. Your old man and Jerome's old man would have just written another cheque and not noticed the difference! Talk about spoilt. Bad spoilt, too. You were both smoking by the time you were fourteen. Okay, I know a lot of kids do, but they don't have their cigarettes bought for them by their parents! Jerome did. You, too, I think. I can remember John Winter giving Jerome a couple of packs of Marlboro – and that would have been two years ago before J. had even turned fifteen. All he said was, 'Don't tell your mother', and then he winked. Should have given him a clip round the ear, if you ask me. And you know as well as me that Jerome even had a little fridge in his room – for BEER! That's only little things. You had guns, real guns, since you were kids. Well, airguns when you were little but you had rifles from when you started high school. So, all right, you got taught how to use them properly and all but that's not the point. The two of you always had more clothes, the right clothes, than anyone else. I reckon that between you and Jerome you could have clothed just about every guy in the class and still had plenty left!

But that's not really the important stuff. *Kind and decent!* Oh, yes? Given you were just about twins, the two of you, I guess you are calling yourself the same? Sorry, Marco, can't let you away with that. Do kind and decent guys do to Nathan Smart what Jerome Winter and Marco Petrovic did? That's all I'm going to say, Marco. Just you think about it. Look, I know that you and I are really hurting, Marco. We have lost someone we really loved and who, I guess, loved us. Does it matter how it happened? Even that is probably beside the point – the most important thing is that we are honest to ourselves. We have to be honest. I think if we are honest we give ourselves a better chance of, well, not perhaps getting over it, but at least coming to terms with it.

Having said all that I can't put all my stuff in the same letter, so I am stopping this one here and writing a separate one about me and what's happened.

Take care,

Kate

## KATE WRITES A SECOND LETTER TO MARCO

Well, Marco, you asked what's been happening here. Quite bad stuff, I guess. I won't go into it all just now but I'll give you a quick run-down. Lake City, Minnesota, is small. Less than ten thousand folk. Small town America. I know Atherton isn't that much bigger but it seems different somehow. A different town in a different country and all that. If you've seen that movie *Fargo* (and I bet you have!) it's a little like that. My host family, the Johansons, speak like they do in that flick. A long time ago they were Swedish and German.

They're quite well-off, the Johansons. They own a chicken slaughter-house. I don't want to get started on that, it is just so ghastly. They process elderly chickens, old hens that have stopped laying eggs, for a firm that makes chicken-extract type stuff. I will NEVER EVER EVER eat another chicken – not ever again!! There's Mom and Pop Johanson and two kids. Pearl is my age and she hates my guts. Pearl has a few problems. Well, to be honest, Pearl's got heaps of problems! Pearl doesn't seem to want to do anything at all about those problems! We do some of the same classes at the high school. Pearl hasn't got any friends and this is not at all surprising. She is a nasty little bitch and, God punish me for saying it, ugly as hell. It is not my fault that I look a little bit better than Pearl. I lie – I look a helluva lot better and it sure isn't hard to. Now, I should feel bad saying all this stuff, but, Marco, because of what she's like, well, I don't! Enough said. You get the picture?

The other kid is Bull. Not quite a kid – except in the brain department – he's twenty. Bull Johanson. Twice as big as you or Jerome. Short, brushy flat-top hair. Stinks of stale sweat, cigarettes and beer. Bit like you and Jerome after a good (or bad?) night!!! Bull does the dirty work down the slaughter-house – and loves it. Bull's biggest kicks are telling us how he's screwed the neck of some poor old hen that thought it'd got away! You get the picture? Bull was the star something-or-other on the high school football team. He hurt some nigger (oh yes, they call them niggers!) player last week and was doubly pleased with himself. Some of Bull's mates call him Killer! He loves that, too.

Mom and Pop J? Well, I've tried to like them, I really have. I guess they can be forgiven for thinking crazy Bull, their son and heir, can do no wrong, is God's gift to everything. Yeah, *everything*, and that includes me! They are a lovely family (not). God knows how the Students Abroad Foundation ever picked them as a host family. I think it was because when Bull was seventeen he did an exchange

– to South Africa, and he sure as hell didn't stay with a nigger family! I guess, on the face of it, the Johansons would look okay – if no one had the time to dig beneath the surface. Nice house, nice cars and all that rubbish – and they're pretty big in some crackpot church! It's hard to spot any bits of church teaching that have rubbed off on Bull and Pearl.

Now, I suppose I could have put up with the old hen killing, and maybe I could have put up with horrible Pearl, but I cannot put up with Bull! I should have had that bastard charged with statutory rape! Sometimes I think that may be the only reason they are hosting me – as cannonfodder for Killer. He'd wait till his olds were away to some church thing and then go for me. The last occasion I'd had enough. Bull cornered me – half drunk, as usual, something the size of a tent-pole poking out of his baggy shorts. I did the only thing I could. He got my very long fingernails right in, on and around the only two sensitive bits of his filthy body. I had no idea that tent-poles could shrink so quickly! That's all, really. My only joy for the next few days was the sight of Bull waddling around like a disabled crab (he had to go to the doctor – hee hee!).

Unfortunately Pearl caught the whole horrible scene and I got landed in the shit every which way. It is all my fault. I am a painted hussy, a temptress, a whore of Babylon and a slut. As Jerome always said, shit happens. Mind you, they could hardly get rid of me. Who would believe poor Bull? I got rid of them – and it has taken some doing. There was a whole heap more crap that happened and it got very nasty. However, Susan, bless her, got John Winter – bless him, too, and I haven't often said that – on my case from the home end and now, thank the Lord, I am off and away. Nothing, nothing could be as bad as these first three or four months. Can't wait to get to Minneapolis and my new family. No more for now. I'll tell you the rest of it some other time.

Kate

PS. Once I'm at Jills and Sally's I can e-mail. Had a letter from them today. I go to them when they're back from some conference in Italy.

---

## MARCO WRITES TO KATE

Dear old Katie,

You sure as hell haven't changed! You've given me my first laugh for god knows how long! Poor old Bull! You nasty bitch!! Oh, Katie, I can just see the poor bugger! I am having another laugh right now – man, I wish Jerome was with me. God he'd laugh. I can see old Bull trying to walk around. OUCH! Bet he didn't catch too many old hens for a coupla days! Oh, tee hee. I wonder what bits the doc bandaged? I can see it now! 'I am sorry, son,' says the doc. 'Too small to get this Bandaid to stick proper. Can't you get it up a bit bigger?' Oh, how sweet. You did well, Katie. Good on ya!

I am sorry you have had a bad time. That's all I can say. Me? I'd never do one of them exchange things, anyway. It's like you're being spied on all the time. We had one at school last year, remember? Nice guy. Micky something from Switzerland. Hope your new family are heaps better. Have they got any kids?

Okay, I've stopped laughing. What the hell d'you mean about Nathan Smart? That jerko geek was a poof! All Jerome 'n me ever did was point it out to him! You got all that wrong, Katie. That guy got on everyone's nerves with his poofy ways and it was a damn good thing he left. We never did anything real bad to him. You remember some strange things, girl.

Glad you got e-mail where you're going. I got heaps of time these days – I can e-mail you every day or we could even chat if they got a chat line set up. That'd be kewl! Got my own computer now. It's a good bugger. Was at Dad's work but a bit small for all the stuff they do so he's given it to me. Spend most of my nights now cruising round the Net. Shit, there's sure some hot stuff floating round in space! You wouldn't believe it, man. Just wish Jerome was with me to share it. His old man hates computers and would never let him have one. Well, actually, old Winter said he'd buy one for Jerome if Jerome learnt to read first! God, that was a bit unfair. Jerome could read as good as me, well, nearly. Just that he never saw much need for straining the old eyes if he didn't have to! Did he ever tell you, Katie, how we were gonna leave school at the end of this year, get jobs, save like hell and go into a business of some sort? Yeah, that was the plan. What will I do now?

God Almighty, why did it have to happen? Why?

I was trying not to write about Jerome in this one. He's with me all the bloody time. I stopped telling him to piss off. It's like that old movie, *Ghost.* It's just like that. I just wish him 'n me could make contact like the guys did in that – well, the girl and the guy. Guess it only happens in movies and fairy stories.

Well it's just my old man and me now. It's not all that kewl but it's not all that bad, either. He's okay, my old man.

No nagging. Well, not too much. He has made me get off Jim and Jack. Reckons seventeen is a bit young to be belting it back as quick as I was. I think he's wrong. I reckon seventeen is just the right age! However, he says he'll buy all the beer I want if I give up on the old J&J for a while. Who am I to argue? He doesn't give a stuff about me smoking because he smokes a helluva lot more than me. We got a woman coming in every second day to clean the place and do the washing and stuff and an old guy comes around to do the garden and lawns. Nuthin for Marco to do – and that's sweet by him! Dad 'n me eat out most of the time and when we stay home he just gets whatever stuff we like sent in. It's a good life, eh?

Yeah, all sounds so fuckin sweet but it isn't. It's dead boring and our house is as quiet as Jerome's grave unless I got my music going – and, oh Jesus, I can't play that without wanting to scream because of who chose most of the fuckin stuff and every second sound just brings him into the fuckin room with me. Our house is like the grave all right and I wish Mum and Cherie and those fuck-awful cats were back here and Mum nag nag nag at me about what I should be doing. Must be losing it, Katie! Shit!

Dad says him 'n me are flatmates. Do you know what, Katie? I don't want a sodding flatmate, I want a sodding father! Now I've said it – at least it'll save you from saying it.

Like what guys do you know have fathers only seventeen years older than them? Sweet bugger all is what. And my father? Looks bloody ten years younger than he is and I look a bit older than I am and anywhere we go everyone thinks we are brothers. And we are not brothers. He is my Dad. Like he's never gonna do father things with me now like Dad and his kid going fishing. Not likely! This father and son do the bars, the clubs and the pubs! And we all know what he was up to when he was younger than I am now. Getting Mum pregnant when they were both kids! You reckon Jerome 'n me were wild. What about my olds?

I love him. Guess I love her, too. I do. Like they sure have given me everything I ever wanted – you were right there. They were never, ever mean. But you know what he said to me last night? Dad? He said, 'You want to bring home a girl and score with her, man, that's fine by me. What goes for your old man goes for you, too,' and then the bastard gave me that wicked grin of his, and a big wink, and said, 'I'm just prayin' you'll be a bit quieter in the sack than your old man!' Jesus! I sort of love him and hate him at the same time. I know he gave Mum a bad time and that's why she's as bitchy as she is now. I hate it when she looks at me in a certain way because I know she is just seeing him and what he's done to her – and that is not my fault.

I'm not stupid, Katie. I know most guys'd give an arm and a leg to have it as sweet as me. Marco Petrovic must stop complaining! It's a cool life!

Gotta go. My 'big brother' is due home from the factory and we are off out to eat – yet again.

Love ya,

Marco

PS. Your new 'family' thingy. Sally and Jills. Is Jills the man's name? I know Americans have weird names but…

PPS. Do you think Susan would mind if I called round and said hi? I know she never thought much of me and Jerome but it's different now. Funny, eh? There's your Susan and she's your sister and she looks like your mother and then there's my old man and he looks like my bloody brother! It's a mad world.

## KATE WRITES TO MARCO

This is a very quick one, Marco. I'm packing. THANK THE
LORD I'M PACKING. I lie. I have already packed and I can't
wait so I may as well drop you this quick line. I AM SO HAPPY
TO BE OUT OF THIS PLACE!

They've left Pearl to check I don't flog the family jewels
(and I don't mean the little I left between Bull's legs!). Jills
is coming at four. I told the Js I was writing a couple of letters
home (done one to Susan already) and Pearl is to see I leave
the money by the fax machine. It's ten in the a.m. and Jills is
driving up and should be here at four and my co-ordinator is
coming, too. My e-mail (Jills told me they got me an address
and I can change it if I want) is katie22@hitmail.com. Do one
to me there and let me know yours.

You and Jerome made Nathan Smart's life hell, Marco.
You terrorised him so horribly he didn't know which way to
turn and if you don't know that, well, there's not much hope
for you. I loved Jerome and I like you but I am not going to
let you whitewash yourselves on this score. You drove that
poor guy to the point of suicide. You call him a poof? What
do you mean? Was it his soft voice and his soft look? Was he
just easy game like some poor rabbit? For two years you and
Jerome gave him no room to move, nowhere to go and there
was no way I could get either of you to listen – least of all
Jerome. Now don't you bloody write back to me and tell me
you never laid a finger on him. I know you didn't – well, not
that I saw. But you did worse. What you did to Nathan is

probably more evil than what Bull Johanson does to anything smaller and weaker that gets in his way – like, that creep just bashes them up, squashes them flat. Bull would have been expert at forcing arms up little kids' backs or shoving them on top of lockers – that sort of mean shit. Things you and Jerome never would have done. Oh, no. You two used far more cunning. In the end, and I was there – remember? – Nathan couldn't open his mouth. You just think about it, Marco. You think hard. You've got the time and just about the intelligence to work it out. What did you mean by poof? Gay? Is that what you meant? Do let me know. I wonder what Nathan is doing now. I hope he is okay. I hope he is happier than you and Jerome ever let him be.

Yeah, I know. I am being tough. Yeah, I know things are sore and tender for you at the moment. You'll survive. Nathan Smart very nearly didn't.

Of course you can go and see Susan. She'd like that. Susan never disliked you or Jerome. She just saw the two of you as spoilt brats. Can't blame her for that, Marco – she was right! She's flat out. She's running old Winter's office right now – he has given up a bit and also he's having to spend time with Edith. Please make an effort to call on Edith. She might still turn away if she sees you, but then, on the other hand, she may not. You know her well, Marco. God, sometimes she seemed to be as much your mother as she was Jerome's. You are not the only one hurting.

Just a last bit. Jills is a woman. So is Sally. They have lived together for I don't know how long. Can't wait to get there – to them and to the city. Sally is a book editor for a small publisher and Jills is an actor in a comedy theatre company. Should be an interesting life. You can believe me when I say I would have swapped places with you at any moment over the past three months – your life with Daddy sounds like heaven compared with mine.

Get out, Marco. You and Jerome were not Siamese twins and it is no one else's fault that you two shut out everyone else. You were so close. Give one or two other guys, or girls, a chance. I can think of six or eight who are probably just waiting to give you a hand to get over things. He was selfish, Jerome. He kept you from anyone else – and you are still letting him do that.

I am sorry for being so tough, Marco, but that is the truth! Give me a day or two to settle in and then we'll get the e-mails flying back and forth. God, I can't tell you how much I am looking forward to getting shot of this place and into a real city. I know it is going to be everything I want – and need!

All love,
katie22@hitmail.com   XXX

---

## MARCO E-MAILS KATE

Hi, Katie22, and welcome to your new home. Gonna do you quite a few e-mails in a row because I like doing them and now I got someone to e-mail to! Hope you like it in Minny-whatsiname. My e-mail address which will come out on what I send you is

bigballs@ibuzz.co.nz
See ya,
Marco

## MARCO E-MAILS KATE

So what? Nathan Bloody Smartarse fucked things up for himself. Of course he was bloody gay. That's what poofs are you know. Smart was the sort of jerk who just made ordinary guys see red and that's why he got it – not that he ever got very much – from me 'n Jerome. We hated him. We done no wrong, Katie, and I don't think he was gonna top himself. You are being dramatic. See ya.

Marco

## MARCO E-MAILS KATE

Yeah, I'll have another go at calling on Mrs Winter but I don't know what to say when I see her. Yeah, I will give your Susan a call. Like, shit, I got nuthin else to do. You are gonna get a heap of e-mails. Dad wants to take me over to Noumea for a week. I don't want to go because last time I was there it was with Jerome and the Winters and it was kool, kewl, cool – and very hot in the middle of the day. Anyway, I don't think it's just me he's taking. He's all over his new designer, Marla. Bet she comes, too. She's only nineteen and just out of design school. She thinks she's in heaven designing dirty T-shirts for Daddy. Reckon I'll have to call her Mum?

Marco

## MARCO E-MAILS KATE

Hey, Katie, I been thinking. Your new 'family'. Are you sure they're okay? You got me worried. A couple of women calling themselves a family. Sounds very odd to me, man. I think I'd be careful if I were you – you could be jumping out of the frying pan into the flames. I don't like to worry you Katie, but I have a feeling that these two women you're going to could be queers – you know, lesbian thingies, gay tarts. You just be careful. They could want you for something. You got me worried and I don't know what to do. You e-mail me or phone me back when you get this and just let me know its all right, okay? Jesus, you don't want another place going wrong for you.

    Marco

## KATE E-MAILS MARCO

Dear Bigballs!!

Jills was amazed that so many messages were coming in for me even before I had arrived. It's okay, they don't read them or anything and now, of course, I've got my own password and all that nonsense. I don't care if either of them read anything I write – or what comes in for me. Not that I have a wide selection of people writing to me – just you and Susan. Oh, Marco, you are a much much nicer person as a 'penpal' than you ever were as an almost-next-door-neighbour! I'm getting to quite like you! You can even be funny. Bigballs?? Firstly, I want to know how you've worked that out. Like, have you compared yours with those of others? Do you measure? Like how? Do you all sit round in the changing rooms at school with tape measures? Or is this just a dream, a sort of wishful-thinking dream? Yeah, that's it. Dream on, LITTLE boy!

Marco, it is heaven here! I cannot believe my luck. These two women are the greatest! After five or six hours I think I could stay here for the rest of my life! I feel free. I feel at home. And they laugh, Marco. They laugh and joke – and it's not about horrible shit like wringing some old hen's neck!

They've told me they are the world's worst cooks and the only reason they've given me a home is in the hope that at long last they can eat an edible meal at home. Poor fools! They'll soon find out! They'll soon be sick of spaghetti bolognese! Sally told me she wants good Kiwi cooking – she spent a year in New Zealand as an exchange student a century ago – and she says she is looking forward to roast lamb, mint sauce and pavlova every second night. If only Susan knew she'd be in stitches! So we ate out tonight. Don't worry, Marco, you're not the only one who's gonna be dining out all the time! Roast lamb, for Godsake!

Oh, they are just such a happy couple, you'd never believe the difference between them and the Johansons. I won't say any more bad things about the Johansons. I think their ways and thinking are all wrong but I suppose it was good for me to see another side of American life. Pearl said goodbye to me quite nicely – I think she was pleased to see the back of me! It must have been hard for her having me around. Life is an uphill battle for someone like Pearl at the best of times and I've been mean about some of the things I have said. I just think that what they think is all wrong. Enough said.

It's okay, Marco, Sally and Jills are a couple. Yes, they are lesbian. Call 'em dykes if you want to. They have been a couple for over ten years. No, they don't want me for any kinky reasons. I am quite safe with them – a helluva lot safer than with Killer J!

They are most certainly not 'closet' queers. They are a well-known and very successful couple. I knew this, the exchange people know this and Susan knows this. Don't you worry your pretty little head, Bigballs.

Start the new school Monday. Not looking forward to it but it can't, just can't, be as bad as Lake City High. Sally says they've a wonderful drama department (which suits me a-okay) and a terrific track and field team. I sure hope to make this and get properly back into my jumping. I'm off for a run with Jills in a few minutes so I'll sign off and send this.

Take care, Marco. I'll write again in a couple of days and talk about YOU and not ME. In the meantime, get out that tape measure, do a bit of checking and let me know the actual measurements of you-know-what!

K.

## MARCO E-MAILS KATE

Dear Katie,
I don't care what you say, gay people got no right doing shit like looking after kids even as old as you. I think it is all wrong and if I was you I'd sure be very careful. What the hell would Jerome say, his woman being looked after by a coupla queers? It's wrong, mate. It is all wrong and I am worried. Jesus, I can just hear Jerome on this one. He'd go ape. Dunno whether I should go and see Susan. I can't believe that your Susan knows about it? She can't – or if she does she sure don't know what it means or what they might get up to. If you were a guy I'd tell you to sure as hell keep your back to the bloody wall but I don't know what to say to a girl. I don't. At least bloody old Bull did it normal – or tried to! I've said it once and I say it again, Katie, IT IS ALL WRONG.

I'm only gonna do you this one e-mail right now 'cause I'm so stewed up.

Marco

## MARCO DOES ANOTHER E-MAIL TO KATE

Yeah, well, Katie, I'll do you another one because I've got nuthin much else to do and I've had a bit of a think. I know you don't like them, but I think maybe you would be better off back at the Johansons' in the meantime. They weren't all that bad and they were safer. There's nuthin wrong, man, with screwing old hens' necks and there's a helluva lot of people who talk about niggers. Plenty of guys at school talk about niggers – when there's none of them around. After all, they talk about us the same way and call us honkies. I do think, Katie, you should be thinking about what Jerome would think. You 'n him, Katie, you were the coolest couple in the whole of Atherton and everyone said so. Don't you reckon you are letting him down?

There's one other thing. You got me very worried about Nathan Smart so I did some checking and a bit of spying. I still dunno what you think me 'n Jerome did to him or why you think it was so bad. Sure doesn't seem to have harmed him. I parked the car (Dad's given me the little Daihatsu) just along from the Smarts' house and spied just like you see in the movies. I ate three Big Macs and had a thickshake while I waited slumped down in the front seat – at my size in the Daihatsu it wasn't easy. Well, Katie, he's sure as hell not dead! He came out on the front steps with another guy and they sat down and had a beer each and I think they had a smoke and they both seemed quite happy. And you know what? You'd never guess, man. Nathan Smartarse looks quite normal nowadays. He's grown about half a bloody metre and put on some weight and he's got rid of those dorky glasses and he looks just like a regular guy!! It is amazing, Katie. Now he looks like the sorta guy who could be a mate of mine – well nearly good enough. I was just bloody staggered. Whatever Jerome and me done to him musta helped, eh? Not that we did do anything. You know, Katie, I guess time changes us all. It sure as hell has changed Nathan Smart in very good and surprising ways.

That's all. Now for Chrissake get out of that place, Katie, before it is too late. Please. Think it over and think about what I said about the Johansons. They were an almost okay family. I am thinking of you and I am thinking of Jerome and what he would say. I know it's not your fault and I'm sure if they knew the full facts the Johansons wouldn't be too pissed off to have you back – at least till they find you a proper family.

Take bloody good care, mate! You know what I mean.

Marco

PS. There is no need for me to do any measuring. I know what I got. I know it's good. I know it's in the right place!

# KATE WRITES TO MARCO

Marco:

Sending this as a fax. It's easier for me to type it up, print it off and send it that way, knowing I've said things the way I want to.

Drop dead, mate, on any number of counts. I know where I am. I know why I am here. I know what I am. Okay, so I haven't told you the whole story. Too bad. Most of it is my own business and any shit I got into was my own fault. However, I will tell you. We have got much closer than I ever thought we could – and this is because of what happened to Jerome, I know. You've helped me through a bad few weeks and I hope I've helped you a little bit. As much as we ever can be, Marco, I guess we are 'mates'.

Marco, I am gay. There, I've said it to you. I'm OUT!! To you and to the whole darn world. I am living with Sally and Jills because I am gay. The Students Abroad guys were sensitive enough to my situation to work out this was a good place for me to be and good people for me to be with. I also know now, Marco, that this would have been an equally good place for me to live and stay if I had been as straight as you think you are! Sally and Jills don't want me, Marco, not in any kinky way you've thought out in your strange little mind. Jesus, they've got each other – and they are happy that way. They are a perfectly normal and very happy couple and I know I am going to love being here with them. So, mate, stick that up where the sun don't shine – in that little hole just up behind the bigballs!!!!!

Yes, Marco, I am a dyke. That's what landed me in it up in Lake City – not that I meant it to. Even I could work out it was not the sort of place for a kid like me to 'come out' in!! It was a chance thing. I said something stupid to someone at the school there and all hell broke loose.

Yes, I was the homecoming queen – and that did nothing for poor Pearl, let me tell you. I didn't really want to be. It's a strange ritual thing that high schools and colleges have here. The homecoming king, my 'partner' was the school stud, Matt. A nice guy, really. Very nice. Reminded me a bit of you. My homecoming 'princess' was a girl called Verna. A real beauty – she should've been the queen by rights but I guess they were being nice to me in a sort of way. Anyway, some stupid twit said to me how lucky I was and that she would have given her eye teeth to have been partnered and later screwed by Matt the hunk. Off the top of my head I said something very, very stupid. I said to her that she was welcome to Matt, she could have him, and that I would give my eye teeth to go home to bed with Verna. I could have killed myself as soon as I said it.

There. That's all. That's all it took. The whole thing spread like wildfire. It blew way out of proportion and stupid thick dumb Kate was well and truly in the dog-droppings. Next thing old Bull took it upon himself to 'straighten' me out, and, well, you've heard that story. In a perfect world such things would not happen like that. Lake City, Minnesota, is not yet part of a perfect world. To be fair, much the same would have happened to me at home in Atherton. Just think of what you've been saying to me, Marco, and how you have said it! That is Atherton. That is Lake City.

I think that is all I want to say. I have given you enough to think about. I wonder if I will hear from you again?

In case I don't hear again, just let me say one more thing to you. How lovely for you that Nathan Smart has turned out well. How good that he looks 'normal' and almost up to your friendship standard. How nice that he's filled out and grown up and got rid of the specs and found a mate he can drink and smoke with out on his front porch. Do you ever think about what you are saying, Marco, before you say it?

Well, for Nathan's sake I'm very glad he is no longer little and weedy and nice and ready and ripe to be a victim. I'm glad he has almost reached your standards, Marco. Maybe what you and Jerome did to him helped him after all? Maybe you and Nathan could have a beer and a smoke together sometime and talk over old times!!

Kate

## MARCO E-MAILS KATE

Dear Kate,

I tried to phone you but all I got was the answer machine at your end and I sure as fuck didn't want to put what I gotta say to you on that! No way!!

I am going to be very calm and very cool. I can't afford to let my true feelings get in the way. YOU ARE NOT GAY, KATIE. There is no way someone who looks like you could be gay. It is all in your imagination. There is not a guy at school who has not lusted after you and talked real dirty about you. Look, Katie, you look better, ten times better, than a real-life Barbie doll would look. I mean that. You are a BABE! You are a number one top BABE – and babes like you are not queers. Ask anyone, man.

Katie, all of this shit is in your imagination and it is up to me to help you with it. I went round to talk to Susan but she was away for the weekend. I didn't want to worry her but I thought it was best that she knew and it was best that it came from a friend of yours like me and not from an enemy – and you sure got a few of them, Katie – well, you would, given the way you look!

I'll tell you what I think. I think it's all because of Bull Johanson. I reckon that guy must have been so gross he put you off other guys for a while and you started imagining things. He has a lot to answer for, Bull Johanson, and I just wish that bugger'd stick to screwing chicken necks and not babes like you. You have had a bad experience, Katie, but it's not too late to save yourself – just remember that. I'm here and I am always available for a chat – one way or another. I feel responsible for you in a way, what with Jerome not here.

Can you just think about Jerome for a mo? Can you just think what he might think? Give it a go, Katie. He was your guy and you two guys loved each other – you said so. I know so! I'm not going to go into what Jerome might have said and done if he knew all this – that would be too painful for you and for me. But we both know in our hearts what he would have said and how he would have acted.

Okay, maybe I was a bit rough about your new family. They do sound like nice women in spite of everything. I must give them that. But, Katie, you know and I know and the whole world knows that what they do and how they do it is not what God meant us to do. I don't wanna get all religious because you know I don't give a stuff about what God says, but sometimes it's gotta be said. You know, you've had me so stewed up I got through a half a bottle of Dad's Southern Comfort and I'm not happy about that because I don't want him to stop my free beers. It's your fault, girl!

So, what I am saying is, I think it would be okay for you to stay where you are providing you are very very careful and don't get contaminated by what is around you. Just keep in the back (and front) of your mind YOU ARE NOT GAY – no, don't quite mean it that way. You gotta say I AM NOT GAY (well I know I'm not but I mean for you to say that to yourself many times a day).

In many ways you don't suspect, Katie, I am quite bright. I know what a liberal is and I know I am one of them. I don't wish harm to any person living or dead who is different in some strange way but even normal liberal people find it a bit hard with queers and poofs!

So you can see, Katie, that I am not mad with you. This is just something you are going through like a bad disease and I know you'll come out at the other end. It has done me good to write a sensible letter on this subject and I hope it will help you. We are friends now, Katie, and I will forget and forgive some of the rude things you've said about me.

Just think about Jerome, Katie. If he hadn't got killed this would never have happened to you, so in a way, and I hate to say this, he is to blame for all this, him being such a stupid bugger. I've thought a lot about him before I wrote this and what I am saying I am saying not only for you but for him. You are a long way from home, Katie (Jesus, this is a long letter, I need another drink) and can be excused for getting it wrong once in a while.

Just had a drink and a smoke and now I feel much more human. You can see now, Katie, that I do understand in a calm way. I am not mad with you. I'm a shitload less mad with you than Jerome would ever have been – mind you, that's okay because you were his woman and it's understandable.

I bet that the next time you write it'll be to tell me you've fallen majorly for some guy in your drama class. Well, maybe not the drama class but at least in the athletics where you find quality jocks with good-size proper balls (ha ha ha). I think your new family would be kind enough to allow you to have a guy around – even if they were jealous.

This whole letter has been about you Katie and not about me. I do hope you appreciate that.

With very good thoughts for your future,

Marco

No PSes because this is serious shit.

Well, just one PS but it is serious. I KNOW YOU AND JEROME HAD A WILD SEX LIFE. JUST THINK ABOUT THAT. A GIRL WHO IS GAY DOES NOT HAVE A WILD SEX LIFE WITH A GUY LIKE JEROME!!

## KATE E-MAILS MARCO

Dear Marco,

Thank you for your letter. I rather thought you might never write to me again. Now, Marco, what you wrote to me was a whole load of crap. So why am I bothering to write back to you? I'll tell you why. Crap you might write but it was all crap that showed you cared about me. Thank you for caring. In some ways I think your letter to me might have been the most caring letter I have ever had from anyone – and that includes my sister Susan! Well, I know she cares and I guess she doesn't have to prove it and often doesn't have the time because she is making a living for the two of us. But, dear old Marco, it is all crap that you wrote and I am now going to take the time to put a few things STRAIGHT.

I am GAY. I am GAY. GAY GAY GAY GAY GAY. Say it to yourself, Marco. KATE IS GAY. KATE IS GAY. Kate was gay yesterday and last year, Kate is gay today, Kate will be gay tomorrow and next year and for as long as she lives.

Some of the things I have to say to you may hurt you a bit. Sorry about that.

I'll try and go through some of the points you make. First, it is nice to know that anyone – male or female – lusts after you. If the guys at school back in Atherton were so darned lustful well, they never really showed it. I'll take your word on the dirty talk! I don't know that I like it, you know, being undressed in the minds of perverts like you – it's hardly a turn-on!

You can blame Bull Johanson for many things but you can't blame him for turning me off straight sex. In the strange event of Bull Johanson being Miss Bull Johanson and coming on at me, well, I would have reacted in just the same way – although I couldn't have gone for her balls!

The guys in my new drama class (and the school is *tops*) all seem quite straight – as far as anyone can tell. There is a real jock on the track team – broad shouldered, blond, great pecs… he throws javelin. His lover plays on the football team and has even better pecs!

I am glad to hear you are a liberal, Marco. It makes me feel a whole heap better about you, now you've told me that!

You are right when you say that Sally and Jills would not mind if I had a guy come round. The javelin thrower, Brad, and his friend are coming round for dinner (spaghetti bolognese!) on Saturday after the game. It wouldn't matter a bit to S or J if they were straight, gay or somewhere in-between. Mind you, Marco, it is nicer if they're gay! Brad and Jon are something else – a bit over-muscled but, hey, pretty good to look at! It's a pity that football jocks anywhere in the world have so little conversation – and Jon's no exception.

I am very unhappy at being likened to a Barbie doll! A *Barbie* doll??

Now, to the big ones.

Susan is my sister and my guardian. She is my half-sister really. She has looked after me, just like a mum, since Mum and Dad were killed when I was eight. She is my family and no one could have a better one. Susan knows what I am. I have to be honest and say that she wasn't very happy when I told her – I was fourteen. She said she was sad for me because she thought it would make my life so much harder. It has made no difference to our relationship. She loves me, I love her. But, Marco, she does know.

And now, the very hardest one of all to say to you. I was never Jerome Winter's 'woman' in the way you meant. Jerome and I never had a wild sex life. Jerome Winter was my very best friend, my closest friend, and I miss him like I can never say. Believe that. What you have said to me, Marco, is proof that Jerome was my very best friend. You see, Jerome knew exactly what I was. He knew all about me. Clearly he never told you – his other close friend.

Jerome protected me, Marco. Okay, I was always known as Jerome's girl. God, that helped in so many ways. None of the other guys was ever going to make any sort of a move on me as long as I was thought to be 'his'. Obviously this was only going to work until I did find someone I wanted. I didn't – well, once I did but it didn't last for long because she was only in town for three months. You'd remember Cassie, Marco? Another Barbie doll? All of this was only going to work until Jerome found someone too. I know this could have happened at any time – for both of us. We both knew that.

Jerome and I often kissed – generally on the cheek! He was my best mate, too, Marco. I loved him. We hugged and romped around and if we went to parties I could drape myself round his neck and act the fool and so on... and none of it was quite acting because we were so close. We shared many secrets, Jerome and me. Shit, I've made myself cry.

The other thing I've got to say is that Jerome's and my friendship never made any difference or threatened his friendship with you. I now know he never told you any of my secrets. Well, Marco, he never told me any of yours – and I know you must have shared a few. Good old Saint Jerome, eh? (cry cry cry – oh where is a bottle of Southern Comfort? Yuck!) I'm no fool, either, Marco. Jerome, as I have said over the last few weeks, could be a right prick, too. He was to me and he was to you!

I'm going to end on a little something that might make you grin a bit – even tho' he probably told you about it. You know how he used to make me go rabbit shooting with him? I don't think he ever had to make you do it – you wanted to! Him 'n me would go spotlighting poor bunnies – up in the old cemetery, yes. I guess I was his 'woman' – I got to hold the light while he shot! I also had to put the poor bastards out of their misery because Jerome couldn't bear the feel of them (you'd know that, too, but probably you enjoyed that bit! There's a bit of Bull J. in every guy!) or the thought they had been down in the 'dead bones'. Well, he was trying out this 'super-silencer' on his .22 – and it certainly was quiet. We snuck around that clump of bushes by the old graves with angels and statues. I turned the spot on full and didn't only spot three bunnies but... Mr Parsons from the gas station and Mrs Harvey from the supermarket – stark naked from the waist down and doing the wild thing right underneath that very big angel with the outspread wings! 'CHRIST!' yelled Mr Parsons. 'She's found me!' Well, Jerome and me just about died from fright, too.

That's all for now, Marco. I don't think you're going to give up on me no matter how much of a shock this letter might be. And I know it will be a bit of shock. Give yourself time to think about things, man. DON'T you dare write back with any hope that you might be able to 'save' me. There is nothing to save me from. I am what I am. I was made that way. I am as happy with the way I am as you are with the way you are.

With love,
Kate
No PSes.

---

## KATE E-MAILS MARCO

Marco:
Four days and not a word. Are you all right? If I have pissed you off for good, well, I will have to live with that. However, I would like to hear if you are okay. Just a yes or no will do and then maybe one line that you don't want to keep in touch. I will try to understand if that's the case.

Kate

## MARCO E-MAILS KATE

Yeah, well, Katie, been sick as a dog, eh. Real sick, crook guts and all. Got the 'flu on top of everything else. I'm gonna write in a day or so when I can stay outta bed for more time than it takes to have a piss.

You'll never believe it, Katie – my old man stayed home from the factory and looked after me. Can't believe it myself – not that he was any good at it! I said what about the factory? He said Dirty T's could get fucked and looking after his boy came first. Cool, eh?

Feel like shit, look like shit, smell like shit, and have got some shit thoughts.

Marco

## MARCO E-MAILS KATE (THREE DAYS LATER)

I'm better. Great what a cup of coffee, a couple of smokes and Dad back at work can do to make me feel better. Dad'll never make a nurse. I think I might have got better quicker without him! Like, he sure stopped me smoking (didn't want to, anyway) but *he* never stopped smoking and the stink – Jesus! And his stereo blasting out olden days crap music non-stop! Every ten minutes he'd come in and check if I was still

alive and wake me up just to bloody make sure. You know I
love him for being worried and all but you'll never guess
what he tried to give me to eat? Fish and chips and bloody
pizza! Nearly fuckin killed me! When I spewed it up at three
in the morning he called the doctor! Thank Christ I am
better now.

Dunno what to say, Katie. I just don't. I never did expect
my best mate to tell me what he got up to with his girl but
this is different. If my best mate got up to nothing with you
and there was a whole load of reasons why not, then I think
the bastard could've said something. See, I just don't know.
He musta gone through hell keeping his hands off you.
Dunno dunno dunno.

I can't think straight. I think I am still sick and I'll go
back to bed and do you another one later. Stay cool,

Marco

## MARCO E-MAILS KATE (TWO HOURS LATER)

I can't believe that Jerome knew what you were, Katie. I know this, Katie. I don't wanna hurt you so I'm gonna put it nice – JEROME DID NOT LIKE GAY PERSONS. I guess this proves what a good mate he was to you letting you tell your shit to him and not arguing with you or talking you out of it. Come to think of it, I don't think the guy really knew all that much about sex 'cos he never talked much about it. Could be he thought you'd be ready for him some day.

I think it is in your mind, Katie. I'm not gettin at you about what you think. Like, you've had a pretty shit life what with your olds croaking when you were little. I reckon that would be just about enough to turn anyone gay! You think about it. Another thing I think is, well, we all have some pretty weird thoughts just now and again but most of us get rid of them double-damn-quick. I think one of those thoughts might have stuck in your mind. You think about that, too. Okay?

I can't get Jerome outa my mind. I can't believe that you 'n him didn't have a wild sex life. I guess I gotta believe it because you'd sure know if you did. You are right about one thing. He knew how to keep a dead secret, that bugger. Least I know he told you no shit about me, not that there's much to tell. Still, I used to tell Jerome all my family shit. Woulda gone mad, sometimes, without Jerome to talk about it with. All the crap about Dad and his girls. That sorta stuff. Yep, he sure did tell me about Mr Parsons and Mrs Harvey. Jesus, what a laugh! Didn't he ever tell you him 'n me caught Mr Parsons getting it off with Mrs SomeoneElse only a couple of weeks before you went to the States? Some bastards never learn!

I don't have to go to school for a week so I'm gonna go and see Mrs Winter. I have made up my mind.

You really reckon that javelin guy and the football jock are gay? I reckon they couldn't be. I gotta say this, Katie – I really do believe this is all in your mind. If those two guys are as built as you say they are – and I can take your word for it because you'd sure know a stud when you saw one – they just could not be gay. Simple as that! People who look like them, and who look like you or me or old Jerome are not made gay. We don't have to be. Still, who am I to know? My world seems to be turning in funny ways these days.

Now I am going back to bed.

Marco

PS. I am leaving school at the end of the year. There is more to life than bloody school and Dad says if I get a job I can leave. Haven't told Mum!

PPS. I reckon 99.9% of gay persons look like Nathan Smart used to look but doesn't now. Just look around you, woman! Gay guys have high voices and look like second-class girls, and the gay girls look like Ms Robertson the deputy principal – the one who rides the Harley. I am not being unkind, just honest. You gotta believe me, I am trying to understand – reckon Jerome would have wanted me to do that.

## KATE E-MAILS MARCO

Marco:
Sorry you've been sick. Sounds as though you've had it bad!
I hope you are feeling fighting fit a.s.a.p. I know you will be
if you give up the beer and cigarettes. For someone who
thinks that looks are so important I am surprised that you
drink and smoke. Beer will very soon give you a fat gut and
if you go on smoking you'll look as old as your father in a
couple of years. Actually I've got that wrong because your
dad doesn't look very old! But you could, and I think you
will. Hee hee – now I got you worried!

Jerome was just the same, you know. Well, of course you
would know. I'll bet the two of you spent hours together in
front of mirrors from the time you could walk! Did you just
admire yourselves or did you pat each other on the back
too? If good looks are everything you are very fortunate,
Marco. I can remember about a year ago at the Winters'
when you and your father were sitting together on a sofa. I
thought then how great the two of you looked – almost like
twins! – with that straight black hair, big green eyes, high
cheekbones and dead-sexy mouths. Oh Marco, I can just
imagine you reading this and feeling good all over! And
right now you'll be wondering if I am telling the truth and
not having you on! Well, wonder on!

You are not going to believe this, I know, but I have never
worried very much about how I look – after all, I don't have
to look at me! How I feel inside me, though, is a helluva lot

more important and right now I am feeling more okay than I have done since I got to America. I feel at home. I feel as if I have come home – which reminds me, I am coming to my home home for Christmas. John Winter is paying my fare. Please go and see the Winters. *Please.* I am only home for a week because of school over here; in case you don't realise (and you probably won't) it's not going to be summer over here and we don't have our long holidays until mid-year.

Why else am I feeling good? I'll tell you. I think I am falling in love! No. I am in love. I think! I don't know. And she sure isn't a Barbie doll, Marco! She is just an ordinary nice girl with an ordinary nice name, Ann. *Ann.* I will tell you nothing more about her now, Marco. If you do write back just do one thing for me – please don't give me any more shit about being gay. Please? Please don't give me any more stuff about why I can't be gay and why people who look a certain way cannot be gay or why people who walk and talk a certain way are always gay. *Please.* I don't want to be nasty to my 'new' mate who cares about me but, my love, most of your ideas are absolute tripe and rubbish and as crack-pot as the ideas those Johansons had about black people.

Go and see John and Edith Winter.

Oh yes, check out a chat programme called RUin. Cute name, eh? If you want to, and if you can, download it. Then we can almost talk to each other!

Jerome never told me about any of your family stuff, Marco. Never. Mind you, I didn't know you well enough to ask. And, let's face it, man, the whole of Atherton knows about your dad and his girlfriends! Sorry, Marco, but that's the truth. I don't think he ever bothered being as careful as Mr Parsons! I think Mr Parsons must have a very busy life. Wonder who he's doing now?

Kate

## MARCO E-MAILS KATE

Dear Katie,

I have done the two things you said. First thing – I went and saw Mr and Mrs Winter. Shit, man, it was hard. I never been in that house since Jerome's funeral and before that I half-lived there. I got in that fuckin door and all I wanted to do was cry, but I didn't. I loved him, Katie, I did, I loved him and he's fuckin gone and it'll never ever be the same, not ever. Sorry about that. I made up my mind, I am not gonna get emotional. I think you could understand, even you being gay and all that – but I'm not gonna mention that again, trust me.

I'll tell you about it. Mrs Winter said, 'Hello, Marco. Do come in. I'll just call… ' and then she stopped and just said again, 'Come in, Marco.' I didn't know what to say and I just stood there. Oh shit. Oh fuck. Then old man Winter came in and, Jesus, Katie, the bugger gave me a big hug and I said don't come too near 'cos I got bugs – and I told them about the 'flu.

It must be pure shit when your one kid dies, Katie. What do you reckon? You know, for the first time ever the Winters treated me like I wasn't a little shit kid and a bad influence. Old man Winter asked me what I'd like to drink so I made the most of it and said Jim Beam. Mrs Winter just looked at me and said she'd put the coffee on.

I still didn't know what to say but it didn't matter too much because they did the talking most of the time. Mrs

Winter goes away for treatments every week for her nerves and stress but she looked okay to me. Put it this way, she looked as spaced-out as she always did and to me she's always looked a bit spacey. I said I heard you were coming home for Xmas and how nice that was. Old man W. said they had talked it over and they knew what you meant to Jerome and you might like to see where he was in the old cemetery, and spend some time with your Susan and with them. I haven't been to the cemetery again since your flower. I can't go. Maybe I'll come with you. Shit Katie, that'll be a fuck-awful Xmas for you! Well, not your Susan. For the first time ever, Katie, I realised Jerome's olds really loved him. Jerome never thought they did. He reckoned they just gave him heaps of stuff – whatever he wanted – to shut him up and keep him smiling. Jesus, Katie, he was wrong. When I looked at them the other day I suddenly realised Jerome was the biggest thing they had. He was their fuckin life. Bloody Jerome! Robbed me! Robbed you! Robbed his olds – robbed them real bad. Must be bloody sad when your olds are as old as Jerome's and there's nuthin much left to look forward to in your life. You know, Katie, the Winters are old enough to be my old man's olds!

I just kept seeing Jerome everywhere I looked and I thought he might even come down the stairs and say howzit hangin man? – just like he always did. But he didn't. I said to them I was sorry I hadn't been around to see them before. They said they quite understood. And, bugger my days, Katie, then Mrs Winter said she phoned Dad every day or two to check up on how I was. COULDN'T BLOODY BE-LIEVE IT! They were just so cool. Not even Mrs Winter minded when I had a smoke. Old Winter wouldn't mind because he was the one got Jerome 'n me started in the first place. I nearly cracked up though when he gave me a carton of smokes that Jerome hadn't got round to using. And that's not all. I got anything of Jerome's I want. *Anything.*

I don't want anything of his, Katie – not this way. I just want him and he's not here. But I guess I'll take it. Like only a fuckwit'd say no to the little Ruger with the infrared scope! They told me to come round whenever and to just say hello and old Winter said if I came when Mrs W. was away we'd have a beer together! Fuck, I should go, eh? Maybe old Winter 'n me could be mates, ha ha ha.

There was a helluva lot more that I can't remember but I will in the future I know. It's just that now I feel sort of sore and sick inside (and it's not the 'flu). I can't write any more down. I think you could say that I feel sorta empty. It's all gone crazy, Katie, and right now I'm glad Dad is more of a mate than a father and we'll be going out to dinner (yet again) and he'll let me have a drink or two or three more than I even bloody know I should have.

Poor Mr and Mrs Winter. I feel sad for them. He might be your hot-shot fuckin lawyer and mayor of this crap town but he lost so much when Jerome got killed. I think that after all Mrs Winter did love her boy even though J. didn't think she did and was always on his case. Tell you one thing, Katie, I'm never gonna have bloody kids. They just bring you misery when they get killed. Take my advice and don't you have any, either. Course you won't be able to, not now you've turned gay. Well, for the first time I am able to say that might be a damn good thing!

Thing 2 – Where the hell did you get that idea I think 'looks' are important?

Thing 3 – I have downloaded that RUin shit. Weird, man. We're gonna talk! But we gotta be on-line at the same time and I know that our times are a helluva lot different. Hope we spot when each of us is on-line. I am 7347582 on it –

that's my number. You will be pleased to know that I am now a shit hot typer. It is amazing what having your own computer does to you. Do you realise, I have written more shit in the last few weeks than I had ever written in my whole life! Even I am amazed. I am turning into a computer geek – ha ha ha – AS IF!!

Ciao (that is something in Greek that Dad taught me), Marco

PS. My name for RUin is (yes you have guessed) Mr Bigballs. When you put me on your user list that is what will come up. Brilliant, eh?

## KATE AND MR BIGBALLS HAVE A CHAT SESSION

'Well, here we are. Let's chat,' she says to him.

'What time is it where you are?' he asks.

'Midnight.'

'Shit! Is it? Christ! You know what?'

'What?'

'It's the middle of the bloody afternoon here. Incredible, eh?'

'If you say so. Can't you type any faster, Mr Bigballs?'

'Doin my best,' he replies. 'My balls keep egttin the way I mean gettin in the way.'

'Take your time. Those e-mails you've sent me must've taken you forever!'

'No they didn't. It's just that this is bloody strange. It's just funny. If we were in the same room we could see and hear and if we were on the phone we could at least hear!'

'That was a long one. I nearly dozed off.'

'Don't be so fuckin rude.'

She says, 'We could invent a short-hand. Quite a few ppl do. That means people. So, how are you?'

'OK. That's shorthand. I'm better now. Back to school on Monday. Wish I could get sick again.'

'Don't be stupid, Marco.'

'Don't you call me stupid. How are you?'

'I couldn't be better,' she says.

'Are you still…'

'I hope you are not going to say GAY? It's not something I take on and off like a sweater.'

'You are thick, now, K. That's shorthand for Katie. I was gonna ask are you still happy?'

'Thank you, M. That's shorthand for Meathead. Yes I am. Seriously. Thank you for asking.'

'When do you get home?'

'Two days before Xmas. Only a bit of me wants to come.'

He thinks, then types. 'I'm lookin fwd to seeing ya.'

'Very good. I'm looking fwd 2 seeing U, 2!'

'Shit hot!'

'You will be home?'

'Too bloody right I'll be home. Dad said we had to go to Mum. I said no. You would be home. Mum and Cherie can come to us if they have to. Stuff her. I wasn't the one walked out on her. I feel a deep need to talk to you.'

'Me too, man.'

'I stuff things up when I write. U know that.'

'You don't do too bad for a beginner!!!'

'Fuck U!!!!!'

'Are you all right, Marco? I am serious now,' she types slowly.

'Dunno. Yes. No. Sometimes. All I can say and it sounds stupid is part of me is… has died.'

'It's not stupid. It's not.'

'I know Jerome has gone and I know I will never see him again and man, Katie, that hurts. Sometimes it hurts so bad I could scream… Are you there? Your thingy says user-away.' He waits.

'I'm back. Just getting a drink,' she lies. She is crying. The small office where she sits and types seems very hot, very stuffy. She feels so alone.

'Well I just lit a smoke.'

'Sorry I went away then.'

'Don't start naggin, woman.'

'Sorry.'

'It doesn't matter… ' He looks at the screen, doesn't know what to type. Smokes for a moment. 'I think I will go now. I don't seem to be able to say much. OK?'

'Yeah, man. Bye for now, then.'

'I can almost see you, Katie. I almost can, but not quite. I think I can hear you. I'm goin now. Gotta have a piss anyway.'

'And I've got to go to bed,' she says. 'Goodnight.'

'Goodnight.'

'You haven't gone,' she says.

'I know I haven't. Seems hard to go, I think.'

'I know,' she says, and flicks out of the screen.

## MARCO -- ALONE

He wastes no time. Pulls on a sweater and a jacket. Late spring but still cool. He pockets cigarettes, Zippo and a packet of ammo, gets out his rifle, grabs his car keys and is out of the house in less than five minutes.

The old cemetery is as ever. Deserted. Out of use now for twenty years or more, other than by the one or two old families of the town who have family plots. His playground. His and Jerome's. A marvellous playground. Castles and forts. Dungeons, dragons, monsters... Ghosts! A haunting place. A hunting place.

Inscriptions known by heart: 'Come on, softcock. Race you to Albert-beloved-of-Freda!'

'Beat you to one-wing angel!'

'Beat you to the fuckin headless angel!'

'Seen three rabbits just by Pauline-rest-your-weary-head!'

'D'you reckon anyone'd mind if we dug up a skeleton? No one'd know, eh? Reckon a skeleton'd look real cool hangin' by my bed.'

Marco parks his car. Shouldering his rifle he walks up the long tree-lined driveway to the cemetery proper. The old trees – elm and oak – are in early leaf. Wind softly whistles. He goes through a brief ritual to check that no one is around. No vehicles, no footprints, no sound other than the breeze. No sight nor sound of visitors. This playing-field is well out of the town.

Marco hunts. Near-silent in his stalking. Stealthy, skilled.

Unwary rabbits are dealt a quick and lethal lesson. No one has been here, he knows that. His prey have grown careless and pay the ultimate price. Three, four, five fall to a sure aim. The unwary that are not killed outright are dealt a swift, matter-of-fact, brutal death. Their necks are broken. Fifteen minutes, no more. A short hunt.

Collecting his trophies Marco walks slowly, reluctantly to that place he has so far avoided.

'Got these bastards for you, mate,' he says softly, and drops the still-warm, dead creatures on the grave of his friend. 'They won't get into your bones. Not these suckers.'

There are no dead flowers now. No white wooden marker. No grave, really. Just a small neat plaque, bronze on stone. 'JEROME MICHAEL WINTER'. And in smaller lettering, 'Son of John and Edith'.

Marco says nothing more. He sits, smokes and then touches, traces the lettering on the little headstone. After a while he stands, picks up the rabbits and, one by one, flings them as far away from this place as he can. Picking up his rifle he allows himself one last look at the grave and then turns from it and walks away.

## KATE – NOT QUITE ALONE

'I thought I heard something,' says Jills. 'Past bedtime, sweetie. Are you all right?'

'No,' a very little voice.

'What's up?'

'Just had one of those chat things with a friend from home.'

'With, oh, what's his name? Mark? Marco?'

'Yes. My mate, Mr Bigballs,' a tight little smile.

'About your friend who died?'

'Yes.'

'You want to talk?'

'No. No thank you,' and then she cries. Great heaving ugly sobs rack her slight body. Few tears. 'Why did that stupid fucking bastard have to do it? I told him it would be all right. I told him. I told him…'

The woman takes the girl in her arms. She says nothing, just holds on to Kate until the sobbing wears itself out, subsides. 'Anything you want? Anything I can get you?'

'Like he got the fuck out of it… but the pain he's caused…' Then, 'Yes. I want to run.'

'At this time of night? On these streets?'

'I've got to.'

The woman sighs. 'What I do for my friends! Come on. We'll get changed. We'll run from here down to the police station and back – ten times if you want! It's well lit and I guess you can trust whatever cops are on the prowl, although

I wouldn't count on it! Lord, Kate! It's nearly two in the morning!'

'I know.'

'Come on, then.'

## MARCO WRITES TO KATE

Dear Katie,

I am a bit off the e-mails. I want to do a letter that I can hold and see when I done it – and even if I do poke it in the fax machine at least it was a letter when I done it. I think you feel you've done something when you do a real letter. I got a coupla questions for you, Katie. You don't have to answer them if you don't want to or if you can't.

You know about you being gay (which I still don't believe you are, not really) – can you tell me a bit about how you know about being gay and how you feel? Did you just wake up one morning and jump outta bed and say, hey, I'm gay? Was it simple like that? If you were gay why did you go with Jerome? Don't gay girls hate boys? How did you get that dead sexy bastard to keep his hands from all over you? Like, Jerome didn't talk all that much about sex but when he did, man, I could tell what he'd be like with a girl. It's funny. I reckon – and I counted – he musta had about ten girls all up. This is just from what he said to me. I dunno how he had them given the time he spent with you and given the time he spent with me. Reckon old Jerome didn't sleep much, that's for sure! All the times he stayed at my place we never slept. We would talk all bloody night. Mind you, then we would sleep about till lunch time.

So what was it, Katie, that made you think you were gay? I am not being nosy. I am interested because now we have got close I would like to understand.

Did you get any help from anyone? Like, fuck, around our way who would you get help from? Who did you talk to? Susan? (I haven't spotted her yet but I'm trying. Jesus, I'm now giving Mrs Winter a hand with her garden and got no time for anything. She's sure no gardener. Knows less about gardens than I do and that's bugger-all!) Where was I? Yeah, your Susan. Was she a help? Did you have an old aunty somewhere? Or didn't you need nobody?

I want to understand you better and get things straight. You are right about me being a dumb shit about some things.

Dad 'n me are not going to Noumea this time round. Dad's working hard at the moment – every bugger alive wants Dirty T's junk for summer. Shit, you should see some of the fuckin words on those T-shirts! Well, not only the words. Seems Marla is quite a good graphic design artist. Some of them come with a warning not to wear them outside your own home otherwise you'll cop it for being obscene. Cool shirts, man. Real cool.

I think I will go to Oz. This guy I met on the chat-thingy is pretty bloody keen and Dad says it's okay by him. Bruce, the Oz guy, reckons the roos are hoppin everywhere this year and we'd have a great time taking them out. Cool. Just what I need, I think.

Mum is going to study to be a teacher. Shit, that's all I needed! A teacher! She never bloody taught me much. One of her cats got run over, ha ha. Wish I had been driving. I used to try but they were too quick, the sods. A teacher – in my family?! Cherie likes her new school. Well, she would.

Cherie is a right good kid for a teacher to have as a daughter.

Let me know when you are coming home.

Haven't been anywhere or done anything except for mowing Mrs Winter's lawns. That sure takes for fuckin ever! I did tell her it would be much neater and easier to look after if they covered the whole bloody lot with concrete and painted it green! It would, too.

Ciao (Think I made a mistake. Think it is French and not Greek. No one's perfect.)

Marco

---

## KATE E-MAILS MARCO

Oh, Marco, you don't ask me easy questions. I don't mind you asking them but I don't know that what I have to say will really tell you much. I hope and pray that this is not some cunning plan on your part – get Kate to talk and then tell her how wrong she is! I will start with the easy bits and move to the hard bits.

No, I did not jump out of bed one morning and say, hey, I'm gay! Maybe some people do, I didn't. No, I do not hate boys. Why the hell should I? Boys are people, too. Well, so I'm told, tee hee. Sometimes I wonder. I have got boys here who are my friends. And no, they are not all gay. Believe it or not, not every straight boy wants to get into your pants! I have to be honest – quite a few do! I am able to look at a boy and admire him if he is good to look at – not that I have ever thought that this is very important. Remind me to have a look at you when I get home. I think I have forgotten what you look like!!

I was thirteen when I got my first period and it was about this time that I realised a few things. At age thirteen I really only had eyes for women or girls. Do you remember that science teacher we had – Beverley Walsh? I fell in love with Miss Walsh. My first love was our old science teacher! God! I would go to sleep dreaming about Miss Walsh. I even managed to get photos of her! I dreamed on into a future where Miss Walsh and I became a couple and lived together for the rest of our lives. My world tumbled down when she married Mr Berger the PE guy! My heart broke. You could say this was just a girlie crush that most girls go through. I knew it was more than that then – and I know so now. About a year ago I saw Mrs Berger. She looked about two years pregnant she was so big! Hadn't seen her for yonks. God, she was enormous and, poor thing, had lost most of her looks. You know what? My heart still jumped inside me like it was trying to get out. I think I still loved her.

I will put it bluntly, Marco, so you understand (and I know you're not thick, but you are a guy!). I have never ever wanted to fuck a boy. Geddit? I have frequently wanted to fuck a girl. Geddit? This does not go down very well with boys. Boys get pretty pissed with girls who they think should be grateful to be poked by a male – especially them! Geddit? It's also not easy when you look like I do, no matter how hard I try to make myself look ordinary. Sadly, I am blonde and I look bloody funny if I dye my hair dark – believe me, I have tried. It seems that I look like the blonde in every blonde joke ever told. But I'm not.

Now – Jerome. I don't know what it was about Jerome that first appealed to me. I always liked him even when we were all little – even though I didn't have much to do with him. One day, nearly three years ago now, he caught me howling my eyes out. Some bastard had come on at me and I had let him have it. I got called a slut, a bitch, and all the rest – just like at the Johansons. Called for everything. I didn't know what to do.

I don't know why I poured everything out to Jerome. I really don't. But, as simple as that, he became my mate. And because girls at fourteen don't have boys as 'mates', he became my 'boyfriend'. All of a sudden I was safe. I guess being safe with Jerome did sort of keep me from finding what I was looking for, but it gave me some peace and, I guess, space to find out more about myself.

Why did Jerome do it? That's not for me to say. I do know that our friendship was a two-way thing. I don't know anything about the other girls you mentioned. There must've been things he shared with you that he didn't with me – and vice versa. But Jerome helped me and I think I helped him. He wasn't a saint, Marco. I have said it before and I'll say it again, Jerome could be a shit – to me, to you, and ultimately, Marco, to himself. He has made us all pay, one way or another. Just think of his poor mum and dad – and they are not all that bad! That's all for now, Marco. I know I haven't answered all your questions but this will have to be enough for now.

Ciao (I don't think it is French or Greek, Marco. Sure it's not Swedish?)

Kate

## MARCO E-MAILS KATE

Dear Katie,
Got another day off school. Dad made me go to the doctor.
He says I am run down and all that shit. Couldn't talk much
to the bastard. Never liked him anyway. Wanted to know
was I worried about anything. I said no. He said was I sure.
Well, fuck knows on that score but I didn't want that old sod
getting into my head and digging in my thoughts. He told
me if I didn't give up smoking I'd pay a high price. I wanted
to say that smokes cost a high enough price already but I
didn't. The bastard phoned Dad and Dad and me did some
father/son shit. Was I worried? Fuck no. Was I sure? Fuck
yes. Would I like to talk to someone? Like fuckin who?
Seemed the doc wanted me to see a head doc. A psychologist (used spell check for that – cool, eh?). I got mad with
Dad and told him I was fine and to leave me the fuck alone.
   Bye,
   Marco

## MARCO E-MAILS KATE AGAIN

That last one was a bit of a shit one to send you, Katie. Here's another. I'm okay. I really am. Do you know, I got real jealous at Jerome having you and never saying anything much. I really did think you 'n him had a hot sex life and went at it like rabbits all the time (but not gettin shot like rabbits, ha ha). You know, I'm seventeen, Katie, and I never had a real girlfriend and never done it with a girl – and if you tell anyone this I'll fuckin kill you. Got my rep to consider. Been out with girls, sure, a million times. I think I been saving myself for the right one, eh.

Thought I got it right with Caroline King. Jerome hated Caroline. Dunno why. The school ball last year when you and Jerome and Caroline and me all went together. Shit, we looked cool, the four of us! Remember? I got half pissed and so did Caroline and we were all over each other and it was great because I was just like Jerome and was gonna score with the second best babe after you in the whole school – and I gotta say here, Katie, there are some guys who reckon Caroline is a bigger babe than you – but I'm not one of them. Jerome just got all quiet and like he was pissed off with me.

Anyway, I took Caroline back to her place and she said wasn't it nice her mum and dad were away for the night and asked me in. Here's me thinking shit like, well, you're in man. So we get inside and all of a sudden I wanna puke because of everything I drunk, I think. Never touched her because of the too much piss. I went home. Didn't see Jerome for three days and boy he was pissed with me – and I don't mean drunk pissed. I thought, well, I bet you guys had a hot night so I told him Caroline and me had a real hot time. Made up all this cool hot shit and told him about it. Fuck, he didn't want to know. Never understood that. I think I do understand a bit more now. He couldn't have had a hot night with you, could he? Not with you being the way you are. I think the poor bastard wanted a hot night but he was being a mate to you. That's unless he dumped you at home after the school ball and went off after some other babe in secret. Maybe he did, maybe he didn't. Who knows now?

There hasn't been anyone for me since Caroline and, fuck mate, we did nuthin! Don't you dare tell anyone that. I mean it. This is private. I been looking, I have. But there's no one round that does anything for me. Just no one. I think it is my depression that I am having.

I'm now gonna tell you something Katie because it is easier to tell you stuff than anyone else (and sure as fuck not a psychologist) and I know that what I tell you goes no further. It better bloody not. Not this bit. You know what, Katie? It will be three months on Saturday since Jerome died and I have not had one hard-on in all that time. That's pretty fuckin bad, eh? I think that's what's depressing me. Hard-ons are pretty fuckin important to a guy when he's seventeen and there's nuthin happening. Used to get 'em all the time. Shit! Sure could be awkward. Never knew what gave me most of them. This is very personal shit, Katie, and I'm trusting you to let it go no further, but I even got hard-ons out shooting with Jerome. I told him and he reckoned I got a problem because he said it meant I was a sadist. Well that was bullshit and, anyway, if I was a sadist, so was Jerome. Saw him with more than a few boners big as his rifle!

Like it sure is a shit thought that your sex life might be over before it even starts! I can't tell this to our doctor. I can't tell it to Dad. Who else can I tell it to but you?

Gotta go now and take my multi-vitamins and other stuff. Maybe they'll help bring up a few hard-ons!

Bye for now,

Marco

PS. Mrs Winter says it would be nice to hear from you. I have told her what you are up to – but nothing *private*. Trust me – but she already knew about Bull Johanson because Susan told her. Dunno what else she knows through your Susan. Anyway, I think you should write her a letter. Hope this finds you well. Saw something on the telly about snow in America up where you are living. Looked fuckin great, man. Wish we got snow here in Atherton. How can you do your jump training in the snow? Be fuckin cold, eh? How is your friend Ann?

M for Marco alias Bigballs-that-are-now-useless.

---

## KATE E-MAILS MARCO

Just a very quick one because I've got to go out with Sally, Jills and Ann to the opera. We're going to Chicago. My first time there except for the airport. The opera is Verdi's 'Traviata'. Really famous singers and the seats cost an arm and a leg. My first ever opera, Marco! Will I be bored sense-less? Will I love it? I think it will be the latter.

Take it easy, man. Please. Just take it easy. I will write a longer one to you tomorrow. Promise. Just one thing, Marco. You lost part of your very own life when Jerome died. You will never forget him and what you and he meant to each other. You were as close as any two brothers. I think you were closer even than that. You did everything together just about forever. Good things and bad things, man. I guess it doesn't matter which – the fact is, you did them together. I have said before that the two of you shut people out from your lives, and that is so true. Now, poor old Marco, you are paying such a high price. Who knows whether you would have gone on being that close – but that doesn't matter anymore because you will never know. You have lost so much and there are not many people around to understand that. Just don't think that you will get over this in three days, three weeks or even three months – and maybe not even three years. For Christ's sake please write to me whatever you want and as often as you want. Say what you like. I promise you that it will go no further.

Must go. Love,
Kate

---

## MARCO WRITES TO KATE

Hi Kate, another fax this time. Only a couple of weeks and you'll be home for a while. School has finished and that sure is good. Dunno whether or not I'm going back. Don't think so. Don't know what to do and Dad's no help. Dirty T's is on double time before Christmas and I never see him. That's okay.

There's something I have to tell you. I can't tell no other bugger, they'll think I'm fuckin losing it. Last night, Katie, I woke up in the middle of the night and sat up like a shot. Jerome was in the room! He was. I swear he was. He was right there and lookin like he always did with that long slow smile of his crossing his face. And this time, he spoke. I swear it, Katie, he spoke to me. Do you know I can't remember for the life of me what the bugger said, Katie. I think it was just a load of that soft sorta sneaky shit he often spoke about things, about people, about what him 'n me might do. He sat on the bottom of my bed just sort of smiling, speaking that soft talk, smoke in one hand and beer in the other – just like fuckin old times. I couldn't move. Was like I was glued to the bed. Well, I was, sort of. After he had gone – and he wasn't there long – I realised my bed was wetter than if I had pissed in it. Shit, man, was I wet! Dripping all over. And shivering. Shivering hot and then shivering cold. Got up and had a shower and wrapped some dry stuff round me and went back to bed. I think I went to sleep, Katie, but I dunno. Seems I don't know much anymore about anything. Falling to pieces, me. Coupla weeks and you'll be around and I'll tell you it all. All of it.

I know, I know, Katie, it was only a dream. Jerome is dead and buried and in his hole in the ground up the old cemetery. That's where he is. Sure as fuck he's not in my bedroom. Dunno whether it was a good dream or a bad dream.

As the time goes by I seem to be remembering more 'n more about Jerome and me. Good shit and bad shit, just like you say. Like only just before I started writing this I was having a big fat grin remembering some of the sorta wicked stuff. Man! Some of it was a bit wicked!

Was remembering the time Jerome and me oh, dunno, guess it was three or four years ago... fuck, we were having fun. Now you're gonna think Jerome 'n me were just as bad as old Bull Johanson! Real cruel dudes. We had caught that monster black cat that used to live over the road from us. Real big bugger – and black as night. Jerome 'n me decided it'd be a cool idea to change him to piebald – like those black and white cows. We each took turns holding the bugger down while the other one painted a nice white patch and then dried it off with Mum's hairdryer. Fuck, it looked funny. We were havin such a good time we didn't hear Dad sneak up on us – we were out in the garage and Mum was away somewhere. I thought, oh shit, now we've bought it! Any proper father would've belted us black and blue and said, 'Don't you ever let me catch you hurting some poor dumb animal again!' Not my Dad! Good old Dad just grinned and then gave us a hand painting tiger stripes all the way down its tail. Jerome thought Dad was the greatest and told him a thousand times he wished he was his father. Can't say I ever said that to Mr Winter.

I don't want to see Jerome in my bedroom again. It is disconcerting – that's my word for the day! But, that's not true, Katie. I think I do want to see him in my bedroom again. Fuck, I reckon I am going mad.

Can't wait to see you, Katie. Can't think of anyone else I want to talk to.

Ciao (Gotta feeling it could be Italian. What d'you reckon?)

Marco

PS. Opera? *Opera*?? You mean the singing stuff? That sort of opera? I do not believe this. America is doing strange things to you, Katie.

PPS. In case you're worried – the cat was sort of okay. Did end up piebald for quite a while. The old woman who owned him took him to the vet and all the painted bits had to be shaved off. Shit, it looked funny. Never managed to get it to come anywhere near our place again.

PPPS. OPERA!!!???

## MARCO E-MAILS KATE

After I faxed my letter off to you I went down town to the
mall to do some Xmas shopping. You'll never guess who I
bumped into. Bloody Nathan Smart. I was right, Katie. That
bugger's sure changed. So I said 'Hi Nathan' and he said
'Hi Marco.' And I said 'Howzit goin?' and he said 'Can't
complain' or something like that. Then he said 'I was very
sorry about Jerome. You must miss him' and I said 'Shit,
man, I do' or something like that. Then I thought to myself,
fuck it, I better say something – just in case you were right –
so I said 'Nathan, gotta say I'm sorry if Jerome 'n me gave
you shit a coupla years back when you were at our school.
Someone just pointed out to me that what we done to you
was pretty crude.'

Well, Katie, he just smiled at me and said 'Thanks for
that.' So I said 'We were just fuck awful kids back then,
Jerome 'n me.' And then I said to him 'Feel like comin round
our place for a beer one night before Xmas?' and he said
'Sounds good' and I said 'I'll give you a bell'.

Isn't that amazing, Katie?

Marco

# KATE AND MARCO HAVE A CHAT SESSION

'Howzit hangin, mate?' he asks.

'Don't know that anything's hanging. I sure hope not!' she replies. 'How are you?'

'Not too bad. Lookin fwd to seeing you.'

'Me, too. Your keyboard skills are improving,' she says.

'Not surprised. It's all the practice I get writing to you. Can only help. I chat with another guy now, too.'

'Yeah? Tell me.'

'Got on to him from the huntin and shootin pages. Lives in Oz. Him 'n me are going kangaroo shooting real soon. He's in the outback where they are a big pest. Cool, eh?'

'Not for the kangaroos.'

'Stuff them. Gonna get myself a roo. You know what they do with the balls off big buck roos?'

'I hate to think.'

'Turn 'em into little purses. Cool, eh? I'll get one for you.'

'No thanks. I'll pass.'

'Tell me about this Ann you like.'

'What d'you wanna know?'

'Are you in love?' he asks.

'I think I am. Shit, no. I *know* I am.'

'What's she look like. She a babe, too?'

'She is the same size as me. We swap clothes and that's cool. Doubled my wardrobe! She is quiet, doesn't say very much but when she does it always makes good sense.'

'Sounds just like me,' says Marco.

'If you say so, Mr Kangaroo Balls.'

'She a blonde bimbo, too?'

'You say the sweetest things! No. She is dark. Ann is very very dark.'

'Fuck! She a nigger?'

'MARCO!!!!!!!!!!!!!!!'

'Sorry. Well? Is she?'

'Ann is black. She is African American.'

'JESUS CHRIST!'

'You're not going to get into racist shit, Marco?'

'I am not a racist.'

'Oh?'

'Course I'm not. I was just surprised, that's all. Never picked you as someone who'd date a black. Is she very black?'

'Oh God! Let me think… um, er… yes she is very black.'

'Jesus! Is she gay?'

'Marco… I can't write down the sounds I am making because I am laughing my bloody head off so all I'll put is ha ha ha ha ha ha ha ha!'

'Yeah, okay. Dumb question, eh?'

'You said it, Mr Bigballs. Now tell me about you.'

'Nah. I wanna know about you and Ann. What do you do? Like, how do you do it?'

'None of your fuckin business.'

'Ha ha ha… it's your fuckin business, eh?'

'Seriously. I want to know how you are? You can leave the smart crap till you see me face to face and that's just over a week now. Minneapolis-LA-Auckland and get in early on Saturday week your time. Susan is meeting me and I'll phone you when I get down home. Okay?'

'Okay.'

'Now I am off to make myself a cup of coffee and when I get back you will have had time to fill up your chat box telling me HOW U R! I'm outta here.'

He types. 'Been to the doc again. But think I'm okay. Cut down on smoking – down to one pack a day and only do a six-pack of beer in a day. I have one in the morning and then two in the afternoon and then three at night. Cool, eh? Gettin on quite good with Mrs Winter now. Think I have just about talked her into puttin down more concrete. She never says a word about Jerome and I think in her mind she thinks he is just away somewhere. Well I guess he is, eh? Except we are never gonna see him again. Don't see anyone else except her (and sometimes him) and Dad. Said no to going to parties and the whole gang from school have been asking. Can't do it. Don't want to. Fuck! How long does it take you to make a cup of coffee?' He stops typing.

'Oh, I have made my coffee and drunk it and I have been sitting here reading a book this last half hour,' she says.

'Smart bitch.'

'The smartest!'

'What do you want for Xmas?'

'You never bought me anything before, Marco. No need to start now.'

'Now is different.'

'I guess so,' she says. 'What d'you want?' There is no chat reply and she waits for a minute and then types, 'What do you want?'

'What I want I can't have.' He types very slowly. 'What I want I can't never have ever again. Not ever.' Pause. 'Dad asked, too. I just said smokes and beer and ammo and a truck-load of each of them. Cool guy is Dad, he just said okay!' A further pause. 'Tell me just one thing about you and Ann… When you are with her, with Ann, how do you feel inside you?' Yet another pause. 'You there or gone for a piss?'

'I am here. How do I feel with Ann? I want to tell you,

Marco, but I can't in this little box. If I don't write it down and send it to you, I *will* tell you when I see you. Okay?'

'Cool as. You go and write it down now. I do want to know Katie and I'm not being smart or any shit like that. See ya soon.'

She sighs, and then types. 'I think I know now that you're not being smart at all. I'll do my best. Yeah. You can get me a Xmas present. You spend some time thinking what I might like and surprise me and I'll do the same for you, man. See ya – like very soon.'

---

## KATE WRITES TO MARCO

Dear Marco,

I am trusting you. I am hoping you will understand. I hope that I am not a fool. I hope.

You asked me to tell you how I feel about Ann. All of a sudden I don't think I can. I don't think I can find the right words – but I'll give it a go. I can sum it up by saying that she is part of me and I am part of her. When I am with her I feel whole. When she is not with me, when we are not together it's as if part of me is missing. I am not silly. I know that we can't be together all of the time and, for now, that is all right. Well, it's all right and it's not all right!

I love the sight and sound of her, the smell of her and the feel of her. I love the life of her, her warmth, her spirit, her very being. She fills me with a warmth that I have not felt before. Do I make sense, Marco? When we are apart I long, I ache to be with her again. I am happy in knowing that if we are not together at any time, well, then we will be again in the not too distant future. Already, after just a couple of months, we seem to know instinctively what the other is thinking, how the other is feeling. We are in tune and we are just so, well, sort of comfortable with each other. We trust each other.

Is this love? I know and I don't know. All I can say is that for me it is love. I am in love. I love. We spend so much time together, Ann and I. And yet, we don't live each other's lives. Now, I know this all sounds sort of away with the fairies so, for your sake, Marco, I'll get down to the obvious and clear-cut sorts of things.

Yes, Ann is black. Black and beautiful. Like most American blacks she is the descendant of slaves. Her family was from Alabama and were cotton-field slaves. They moved north sometime after the Civil War (you had better look that up, Marco) and settled in Minneapolis. Her father is a lawyer (like who in America isn't?) and her mother is a nurse. She has three brothers. Yes, they are all black, too! No, none of them are gay! One is married with a little kid.

Her family knows she is gay. They seem to have accepted this. A nice family and they have made me welcome. I met Ann on the track team. She is a sprinter and a very good one. She should go far – ha ha ha. Athletics is our thing in common. Like I do drama and English, Ann's big things are math and computer science. So, you can see, we don't do everything together. We have not been in each other's lives for very long and so, of course, she has friends, good friends, that I don't really know. We are still finding out about each other. Both of us were very wary at first that everything was going just too well. Could we trust our luck? And the very big one! What happens next July when I have to come home? Well, we just worked out that we would be stupid if we didn't just 'go with the flow' as the saying goes.

You know, Marco, I just love writing about her. Wow! I like being with her, doing things with her, writing about her, looking at her, touching her body, talking with her and, yes, sleeping with her! I am a bit shy talking about this, Marco, and hope you will understand. All I am going to say is that we have had the most wonderful time in bed – I am smiling as I write this, Marco, and most definitely, all I am going to say to you is – just remember, Ann and I are both pretty good athletes!

Oh, what else can I say? You asked for this. I feel good about everything I have got here now – the city, Jills and Sally, Ann. The repellent Johansons are just a memory. And, Marco, for me, the sharpness of the pain I felt when Jerome died is diminishing, getting less horrible as time passes. I know that you haven't come through things quite as well and I think of you often and I hope that we can spend as much time as possible together when I am home. I know it is only a week but I'm sure we can see each other a lot in that time and I will probably piss you off so much you'll be glad to see the back of me!

I said I was trusting you, Marco. I have opened up on a little bit of my thoughts and feelings in as honest a way as I could. I hope you respect that – even if you don't fully understand.

Ann! Ann? "Shall I compare thee to a summer's day? Thou art more lovely and more temperate:" Shakespeare (old English playwright, Marco, dead for yonks!). God Almighty! *Shall I compare thee to a summer's day?* Well, it's the middle of bloody winter here and I could do with never seeing snow again in my whole life! A summer's day? Well, Marco, all I can say is, I must be in LOVE!

And love to you,

Kate

## AN EXCHANGE OF SHORT E-MAILS BETWEEN KATE & MARCO

Dear Katie – thank you for telling me about Ann. You can trust me and I will not say smart shit about anything. I am glad that you are happy. Jerome would be, too. Just watch out that you are not "a pair of star-crossed lovers". That's Shakespeare, Katie, some old guy dead for yonks. And I seen the movie. Cool, man.

    Marco

Marco: I am impressed. Now read the play. Thanx for your e-mail.

    Kate

Dear Katie very pretty Katie please Katie, I got you a Xmas pressie so would you please get me a duty-free carton of Marlboro Reds (they are cigarettes) and I'll pay you when you get here? Second thought – get me two cartons, the customs'd never check someone like you.

    Love,
    Marco

Marco: No!
    Love, Kate

# KATE AND MARCO TOGETHER     ONE

They are awkward with each other for ten, fifteen minutes.
She tries to greet him with a hug and a kiss. An ungainly
fumble and they break from each other, giggle slightly. They
speak nervously and each talks over the other.

'Geez, Katie, you got thin.'

'I think you've grown a bit, Marco.'

'Still look okay, though.'

'You, too.'

They both look okay. He giggles again, still nervous.
'We're sort of opposites, eh?' He looks her up and down
and then indicates himself. He wears a plain white cotton T-
shirt and blue jeans. He is tanned and his dark hair shines.
She wears a dark blue T-shirt and white linen shorts. She is
pale and her long blonde hair is tied back.

'Okay if I smoke?' he asks.

'Not in here. Susan'd kill me. We'll go out on the back
porch.' She picks up a duty-free shopping bag. 'Here,' and
she tosses it to him.

'Brilliant,' he grins. 'You got 'em for me?' Two cartons of
cigarettes.

'Yeah. And I should be shot for doing it!' She smiles back
at him. 'You owe me forty bucks, our money. God, the money
you fools pay just to kill yourselves!'

'Yeah. Cool, eh?'

'Go on out. I'll bring some coffee. How d'you take it?'

'Milk and two.'

She stands back from him, smiles slightly as she looks him up and down. 'Shit, Marco, you look… you look… beautiful! I had forgotten just how good you…'

'Hey! Hang on a minute. You swapping back from bein' gay or what?'

She laughs, winks at him. 'Don't tempt me, man.'

And then he laughs. They both laugh. The awkward tension between them melts away. 'Reckon we could have a hug now?' and, in absolute silence each holds the other tight. Thirty seconds, a minute… and then she breaks away. Her eyes are moist.

'I'll get the coffee,' she mutters.

'I'll give you a hand.'

'D'you want anything to eat?' she asks.

'Shit no,' he grins again. 'I got these!' he waves a carton of cigarettes.

'You're incorrigible.'

'Sounds like a good thing to be. That an American word?'

They sit on the back steps of her home and drink their coffee. For a while they say little but, for the moment, there seems no need to talk. The sun is warm and Kate leans back, closes her eyes and soaks in the late-morning heat. 'God, this is what I do miss.'

'Why do you have to go back so quick?' Marco asks. 'You could stay longer.'

She sits up and looks at him. 'School starts again on the third or fourth. And I want to get back for New Year with Ann. Jills is taking us skiing.'

'Cool.'

'Cool? It'll be darned freezing,' she laughs.

'Well, guess you'll be back in May or June. You know, after your year's up.'

'No I won't, Marco,' Kate says carefully. 'I'm going to

stay on there for a while. I don't know how long. Might be for good.'

'You can't,' he says, bluntly. 'Us foreigners aren't allowed. I know that.'

'I can. Dad was an American. I have an American passport.' She shakes her head. 'But that's not really why... even though it is how I am able to stay.'

'This is your home,' says Marco. He lights a cigarette. 'You can't just chuck it, not just like that.'

'Marco, it's not a matter of chucking anything. I'm lucky. I can live in two places. Look, these days it's a small world. Here today and there tomorrow. Look at me being here now. There is nothing really for me here in Atherton. Small towns, anywhere, are the same and I'd face the same sort of shit here as I did in Lake City, Minnesota. That's if I wanted to live my life honestly.'

'You could go to Auckland or Wellington. Reckon they'd not be much different from Minneapolis.'

'I know that. But there's more. Susan, at long last, has found a guy who's good enough for her... '

'Poor guy,' says Marco, with some feeling.

'Don't be horrible. I love my sister.' She smiles. 'Yeah. Okay, I know she bosses everyone around but she's got a good heart.'

'I'll take your word for it.'

'Jills and Sally want me to stay on. In no time flat the three of us have become a family and I just hope one day you'll get to meet them.'

'Shit!' says Marco. 'Reckon I'd feel a bit out of it.'

'Rot. There's another thing, too,' she says.

'Your Ann?'

'I wasn't going to mention her but, yes, there's Ann. I love her, Marco. I'm in love with her.'

He looks at her very closely and his eyes hold hers for some seconds. 'I know that,' he says.

'Fuck, man. You have grown in more ways than I ever thought possible.' Kate's lower lip trembles and she bites it with her teeth.

'Here,' he laughs. 'Have a smoke. Steady your nerves.'

'Maybe you're right, but no thanks. That would affect the last reason I want to stay on for a while. I've got a chance of making big time athletics. We've got a great high school coach and the way I've come on he reckons I'll land an athletic scholarship to college – university. In fact it's almost certain.'

'Shit hot!' and he looks at her again. 'Guess you got all the right reasons. Pisses me off majorly but, what the fuck? Reckon I'll be outta here in the not too distant future. Are you sure your Susan's found a guy?'

'Yeah. I met him. He's nice.'

'Bet he has to do what he's told.'

'Of course he does. He's a man! Men should do what they're told. Us girls always know best. More coffee?'

'Okay. I better have something to eat. Haven't eaten since last night.'

'I had better do a Susan on you, dickhead. I've got a week to sort you out. I've got nothing else to do except spend time with you, with Susan and with Mr and Mrs Winter. You know we're all going to have Christmas dinner together up at the Winters'?'

'I know, I know, I know. Fuck, that's the last thing I want.'

'Look at it this way, Marco. It's the least we can do for them, the Winters. None of us was going to have the greatest time anyway. Will your mother be there?'

'No. She's gone to Sydney to stay with her best friend and she's taken Cherie. She hates poor old Dad that much.

Dunno why she has to hate me though. I don't suppose she does but she's only doing it so's Dad doesn't get to see Cherie at Christmas. That bloody sucks, Katie. Fuckin families, I dunno!'

'Tomorrow is Christmas Eve, Marco. In the afternoon can just you and me go to the old cemetery..?'

He looks at her for a while and then looks away. 'Yeah,' he says. 'Good idea.' He looks back at her. 'Now you make me a sandwich, woman! What d'you think you've come home for?'

## MARCO AND KATE TOGETHER    TWO

She brings flowers to place on Jerome's grave in the old cemetery. 'Silly, I know,' she looks at the spray of white flowers in her lap. 'Like, they'll be dead in a couple of days,'

'What the hell are they?' he asks, glancing at them. He drives.

'Orchids.'

'Oh, yeah,' he risks looking at her. 'Haven't been back there since I gave the bastard a bunch of dead rabbits!'

'Let's face it, he'd probably rather have the bunnies.'

'Yeah. Reckon I'll get him another bunch of them for Easter,' he says. 'Easter Bunny. Geddit?' He has brought with him two bottles of almost-champagne, three glasses and a packet of peanuts. 'In case we get hungry,' he tells her. 'Should get half-pissed on the bubbly.'

'What? And then drive?'

'Stop preaching, woman,' and he lights a cigarette. 'Him 'n me could drive up the old cemetery blindfold and full-pissed and still shoot rabbits and then drive back more pissed.'

'I believe you,' she says, winding down the window.

They leave the car at the lower gate and walk the avenue of trees that are now in full leaf. As always, the place is deserted. One or two of the recent graves show sign of some pre-Christmas attention. A few flowers in a jar on one grave. A Christmas wreath of vivid plastic foliage on another.

They both know exactly where they are going and wind a zig-zag path to the back of the cemetery, past Albert-beloved-of-Freda and the headless angel. They don't talk.

Kate kneels at Jerome's headstone, places her flowers. She cries. No loud outpouring, just a steady stream of tears down her cheeks. 'Thanks, mate,' she whispers. 'Thanks for everything.'

Marco pretends to neither notice nor hear. He sits, sprawled on the untidy grass, back against a tree. He smokes and busies himself opening one of the bottles of wine. The popping of the cork from the bottle makes Kate jump. 'Here,' he holds out a glass. 'Hold this and I'll pour. Put 'em on his stone – it's about the only flat bit around. He may as well be of some use.' Three glasses are filled. They each pick up one and leave the third on the headstone. Marco stands by Kate. 'Let's make a toast,' he says. 'To Jerome. Our mate.'

'Jerome,' Kate whispers.

'That's fuck-awful shit,' Marco grimaces and tosses the wine glass away. 'Thank God I put a six-pack in the car. I'm gonna get it.' He begins to walk away from the grave... six, eight steps. Then he turns and looks at Kate. 'Why did he do it, Katie? Why the fuck did he do it?' He hesitates and then slowly walks back towards her. He bends and picks up the empty glass from the grass. Standing above the grave of his friend he yells, 'Why the bloody hell did you have to go and kill yourself? *Why?*' and with all his strength he throws the glass against the headstone. 'WHY?'

'Come here,' she says, very quietly. 'Come here and sit down.'

'I want my beers,' he mutters.

'We'll get them in a minute. Sit down. Come on.'

He does as he is told and sits beside her. Looks straight at her. 'I always knew he did it. I know I got mighty pissed off with you when you said it, but I knew. Even then I knew. Like, well, him 'n me been hunting a million times. That bugger never tripped over nothing, not back then and not when he died. How did you know?'

'I think I knew from the moment I heard.' She says nothing more for a while.

The two of them stretch out in the sun and soak in the warmth of the late-afternoon rays. Marco rolls over and looks at Katie. 'And then? How did you really find out?'

'Susan told me. You know she looked after everything for the first few days. John and Edith Winter didn't know which way was up. She ran the law firm, the office, and when she wasn't doing that she handled the cops, arranged the funeral, the whole works.'

'So?'

'So, well, it was one of those shootings that could have been an accident or it could have been suicide. In the end, she reckons the cops just made a decision that it was better for everyone to go for accidental death. Probably, the Winters being who they are made more than a bit of difference.' She looks at the headstone. 'There was one young cop Susan knows, Mike something, he's a keen hunter apparently…

well, he told Susan privately that he was just about a hundred percent sure that Jerome did it to himself. In the end, well, Marco... dead is dead. He's gone.'

'That's not quite the point.'

'Let it be, Marco. Let him go, man,' very quietly.

'Katie, I can't. I know there's more. I know there's fuckin more and I can't get my head round it. It's like a jigsaw and I got some bits of it and you got some bits of it and that dead bastard's got some bits of it – and, shit, there's probably some bits still missing after all that.' He looks hard at her. 'I gotta know all I can, Katie. I gotta put those bits together as best I can. There is more, isn't there?'

She sighs. 'Yeah. There is more, Marco. And it's going to hurt you. It's going to hurt like hell.'

'I am hurt already, Katie. I hurt so bad.'

'Go and get your beer.' She stands. 'I'd like a few minutes alone here.'

'Okay.' He gets up and starts moving away.

'Marco,' she calls.

'What?'

'You've got a choice, man. If you come back I'll tell you everything that I know.'

'Yeah? And what's the other choice?'

'You get in your car and drive off home. I can walk. I've done it often enough, so don't worry about me okay? I'll see you tomorrow at the Winters'.' She pauses, and then almost whispers. 'If I were you I know what I'd do, I'd get the fuck out of here. But it's your choice.'

'There's no choice at all,' says Marco, and he walks away from her.

# KATE AND MARCO TOGETHER     THREE

'Call that a six-pack? Can't count, either,' she says, smiling.

There is no smile on Marco's face. 'So what? It's a bloody dozen. Just might need 'em, eh?'

'Open one for me,' she says. 'The wine is too sweet.'

'Go on, you can say it. It's cheap shit. Left over from the Christmas party at Dirty T's. Flogged it out of a carton of the stuff Dad and Marla shoved out in our garage.' He hands her a beer and she drinks.

'Yuck, Marco! Hot beer?'

'Stop complaining, woman. It's all we got, the three of us. Cheap wine and hot beer.' He nods at the headstone. 'Him 'n me drunk much worse shit than this.'

'I know.' She goes on drinking.

'Here,' he holds out a small package. 'This is for you for Christmas. Seems the best time to give it to you.'

'What is it?'

'Jesus, Katie! Open the fucker and find out!' He watches nervously as she opens the parcel.

'It's wrapped in... I think it's a piece of silk... ' She undoes a ribbon.

'Sure as shit is. Had to pay for that, too.'

'Marco... ' She has opened it. 'Marco... ' Her lip trembles.

'You don't bloody cry,' gruffly.

'Thank you.'

'It's real solid silver,' he says. 'Not your painted-on shit.

Jerome. Head and shoulders. Tousled head of wind-blown blond hair and a grin from ear to ear. 'Chopped it out of a bigger one. Thought you wouldn't want the rifle he had in one hand or the smoke he had in the other – but it's okay, I got a copy of it.' He looks at the likeness of his friend. 'Reckon that's how I see that bugger. That's his BFG.'

'His what?'

'Big Fat Grin. See!' and he spreads one across his own face. 'Just about twins, eh?'

Kate flinches. She takes her gift and places it on Jerome's headstone. 'There,' she makes it stand. 'Now there's the three of us.'

'Just like old times,' says Marco, but the BFG has disappeared. 'Come on. Let's talk.'

'You didn't have to come back,' says Kate. ' If I tell you all I know you won't feel the same after I have told you.'

'So?'

'Don't shrug your shoulders. This is big stuff.'

Marco looks at the photo. 'If I can just about get through him topping himself, guess I can get through anything.'

'I didn't tell you the truth about one thing, Marco, when we were writing. It seemed, for a while anyway, better not to. I still think it might be better not to.'

'For fuck's sake get on with it.'

'Okay. Jerome protected me, covered for me. I didn't have to take shit from anyone because no one knew – '

'That you were gay.'

'Yep. But… I didn't just blurt out to him that I was gay, Marco. Like, well, what a damn fool thing to do even if we were, well… It wasn't like that at all. It sort of unfolded, gradually. A little bit of trust here, a little bit of risk there, a little bit of not knowing, of uncertainty. Shit, we were fourteen… we were only fourteen.'

'Please, Katie… for Chrissake, trust me. Say what you gotta say. Say what you are trying to say.' He is sitting on the grass, his legs drawn up, looking into her face.

'Marco, Jerome and me covered for each other. Jerome and me were both gay.'

He just looks at her for a moment and then speaks. 'Oh Jesus Christ. Oh Jesus Christ. Oh, please no. Not that. Don't you tell me that. Please.'

'Believe me,' she whispers.

'Oh no he wasn't. No, Katie. No, he wasn't. I know he wasn't.'

She tries to touch him but he pulls away. 'That was the one thing you didn't know, Marco. The one thing he could never tell you… '

He stands and backs away from her. He is shaking his head. 'No!' he yells. *'No!'* louder. 'NO NO NO NO NO!' and he goes on repeating the word and backing off, step by step.

She stands and yells back at him. 'You wanted to know and you would never have let it rest until you did know!'

'I didn't want to know that,' he yells back at her.

'We don't always get to bloody know just what we want to know! We don't always get to hear what we want to hear!'

'Jerome fucking with a guy! I don't believe that!'

'He never *did* fuck with a guy and that was his tragedy, you fool.' Kate is now very angry. 'He never was with a guy, Marco. Never. Not once. There was only one guy he ever wanted, Marco. Only one guy Jerome Winter fucking lived and breathed for – '

'DON'T YOU DARE SAY – '

'Look… ' She points at the photo. 'LOOK, DAMN YOU!! Who the fuck was he looking at with that beautiful beautiful smile across his face and that shine in his eye… '

Marco is cold, he shivers despite the heat of the sun. Very, very slowly he begins to walk back to her. There is no anger, no rage in his voice. It is flat, dead. 'You don't know what you have just done.'

'Oh, I do, Marco. Believe me, I do. I think I know exactly what I have done. For so long I talked to him, to Jerome. The same shit over and over. That he had to tell you. That he just had to tell you. And he would promise. And, then, well, he wouldn't... Please sit down, Marco.'

'I can't.'

'Listen to me. When I left here to go to the States I left Jerome, or so I thought, ready and able to talk to you. He gave me the last of his promises. Do you know, I even threatened not to go away at all if he wouldn't? And then I didn't hear... I didn't hear anything at all from him and I knew that it hadn't happened. And then, when he died, well...' she looks down. 'I just knew that he hadn't been able, yet again, to say anything at all.'

Marco crouches down in front of Kate and speaks slowly without looking at her. 'But he did, Katie. He kept his word, he really did keep his word – and I fucked it up. Was me who got it all wrong... It was me who fucked up. It was me.'

'What? What are you saying?'

His shivering is now a full shaking. 'You know what, Katie? I fucking killed my best mate.'

'What do you mean?'

'I did with Jerome what I always, *always* done with Jerome. I told back to him exactly what I thought the bastard wanted to hear from me. Yeah, Katie, was me who killed Jerome.'

'I don't... '

'He said to me one day after you gone, and yeah, we were up here roamin' around... he said to me when we stopped for a smoke... he said... '

'What?'

'He said to me, what did I think of gay guys – and he wanted an honest answer. He'd never, we'd *never* talked about that shit before. Never. And, Jesus, him 'n me weren't gay. Jesus fuckin Christ. Nearest we ever got to each other's dicks was pissing up the wall competitions when we were little and then when we were fourteen or so a jerk-off or two to see who could shoot the biggest load... Jesus, that was years ago... just ordinary boy, kid stuff. *What did I think of gay guys?* That's what he asked. That's what he said to me – *what did I think of gay guys?*'

'God, no.'

'I let him have it, Katie. I did.'

'I don't need to know.'

'Shit on you, Katie. You told me all this, you may as well have the last bit. Told him just what I thought he wanted to know and we laughed and joked about chopping the nuts off any queer guy who ever...' He is so quiet now. 'A week later he was dead. Reckon I killed my best mate, Katie.' He stands and moves to look down on Jerome's grave. He takes out his cigarettes and lights one, smokes for a while.

Kate doesn't move, apart from an idle plucking of blades of grass. It is still. Almost silent other than the sounds of cicadas, birds and the slightest of breezes through the leaves of the old trees.

'What a fuckin waste, Katie.' Marco turns to look at her. 'What a fuckin waste.'

'I know what you mean.'

'No you don't,' he says, his shaking now reduced to a tremble. 'I don't think you quite know it all. There are three of us here, eh?'

'I do know what you mean,' she says, standing. 'Well, three of us, in one form or another.' A twisted smile.

'Maybe you do know,' says Marco, looking at her now. 'Dunno. It was when you wrote to me, Katie, when I got you to write to me about your Ann... That's when I finally knew. That was when everything fell into place for me.'

She is moving towards him. 'I know.'

'Every fuckin thing you said in that fuckin letter told me exactly how I felt about that bastard down there. Oh, Jesus, Katie... I loved him! I *loved* him! You know what sort of fuckin love I mean!'

Great sobs twist Marco's body and he sinks to his knees. His face is contorted and he is helpless against his agony. His whole body heaves in grief. He lies down and hugs the headstone of his friend, his head on the low, granite stone and his arms clinging tight around the masonry...

Five, ten, fifteen minutes... Eventually Kate moves to him and he curls around and clings to her. And then, worn out, he quietens. 'It's true, Katie,' he says. 'With every bit of my body I loved him. And all the time I didn't understand shit about what that love was. Oh, Katie... ' and he clings further into her.

Finally he pushes away and sits looking, first at the ground and then at the headstone and the picture of Jerome. 'I didn't know, Katie. Honest, I didn't know. Because I didn't know, I killed him.'

'No. No, Marco. You didn't kill Jerome. Jerome killed himself, no matter how you look at it. You didn't kill him. He wasn't quite brave enough, Marco. And God knows, there are times when we've got to be brave and we've got to be honest. He wasn't quite brave enough to tell you... and he could have told you. Jerome could have done it quite simply, just a piece of the jigsaw in the right place at the right time and facing up the right way...'

'How?'

'By simply telling you what *he* was and then seeing how the pieces fell. In the long run he didn't trust you enough.'

Marco looks at her. 'Or maybe he didn't trust himself enough?'

'You're getting it,' she says. 'And then he wasn't quite brave enough to go on living.' She shrugs, tired. 'Or something like that. Neither of us will ever know what went through his mind,' and she looks at Jerome's photo, 'back then when it happened.' She turns away for a moment. 'Everything seemed bleak, black, hopeless...'

'And I will never know what I would have said if he had come right out and said it. Dunno. Might've made it worse,' and he gives a short, savage laugh. 'Except it fuckin couldn't! Oh, Jesus, I was just so blind. Every sign that you spotted in you, as you grew up... every sign that Jerome must've spotted in him and that I guess he shared with you... fuck, they've been in me, too. Never wanted to go out with girls... never. Only ever pretended to kiss one. Sure, lookin' like I do, not hard to get one that looked good – and then, bugger me, never wanting to do anything when I did score.' Another short laugh. 'Poor old Nathan Smart. Jerome 'n me! Jesus. Giving him shit for being what we were. And I don't think he is gay. Brought his girlfriend round for a beer last week. God, it was boring.' He looks at Kate. 'What am I gonna do now, Katie?'

'A lot of thinking, Marco, to begin with. And you've got me. Okay, so I'm off again in a few days but,' she gives a small laugh. 'We've got into the habit of keeping in touch even when we're half a world away. Let's keep that up. I'd like us to.'

'Don't worry. You haven't got rid of me yet,' and he smiles. 'Besides, just might come and see all you dykes over in Minneapolis. Gotta meet this Ann of yours.'

'Any time,' says Katie. 'And... Marco?'

'Yes.'

'All your thinking may not lead you anywhere in particular. You know what I mean?'

'Reckon I do.'

'It might be that what you felt for Jerome stays at just that. Somewhere down the road there may be a girlfriend, someone… shit,' she laughs. 'This is too much. I hope there's a whole heap of boyfriends if for no other reason than that no poor girl deserves to end up with you!'

'Up yours, too.'

Kate goes to the headstone, picks up the photo. She wraps it again in its silk handkerchief. 'Here,' she says, and hands the little parcel to Marco. 'With all my love, Marco. My Christmas present to you.' Her lip trembles. 'It's real silver, not painted. You look after it, now. I'll call by from time to time and check on it.'

He understands. 'Thank you.'

'Come on. We've got to go. Let's clean up,' and in a moment they have.

'You go on,' Marco says to Kate. 'Just give me a minute or two. Car's open. I'll bring the rest of the beers.'

'Okay.' She rests a hand on his arm. 'Just a minute or two.'

She leaves and Marco is alone at the grave-site. He opens a beer, lights a cigarette and crouches down. His fingertips trace the name on the headstone. He has no hope of controlling his tears. 'I'm sorry, mate. Sorry we were both fuckwits, eh?' He has a drink. 'Sorry it came to this. Thanks, mate, for loving me. I loved you too, you know, even if I didn't know what that love was. I loved you, Jerome.' And he turns from the grave of his friend.

Kate moves to Marco from the shadows, takes his arm, and together they walk from the place.